Construction Beauty Queen

Sara Daniel

Entangled Publishing, LLC
2614 South Timberline Road
Suite 109
Fort Collins, CO 80525
Visit our website at www.entangledpublishing.com.

Edited by Stacy Abrams
Cover design by Jessica Cantor

ISBN   978-1-62266-820-5

Manufactured in the United States of America

First Edition September 2012

To my parents, who gave me an inside look at what it takes to run a small-town business. Thanks for loving me despite my mysterious lack of a civil engineering gene. And for Grandma Bonnie: I have no doubt you'll let me know if this meets with your approval.

Chapter One

The checkered destination flag on the GPS screen waved over the entrance to the most desolate trailer park Veronica Jamison had ever seen. She'd faithfully followed the disembodied direction voice for four hours from the only home she'd ever known, with her parents on Chicago's North Shore, to the microscopic town of Kortville in central Illinois. But instead of depositing her on her grandfather's doorstep, the GPS mocked her with its cheerful announcement that she had arrived at her destination.

A man who owned a seven-building distribution complex and had a sizeable investment in a construction company surely didn't live in a dilapidated trailer with duct tape covering the crack in the front window and a partially depetaled sunflower pinwheel struggling to spin in the front lawn. Right?

Then again, Veronica knew nothing about her grandfather, except that he was her only hope for building a life where she used her hard-earned business degree to launch a career that incorporated her financial and leadership skills, instead of existing for cocktail parties that demanded nothing more than empty-headed smiles.

The door creaked on her ancient tank of a car as she stepped out. She didn't think she'd ever get used to the sound, but it was the best she could afford after she'd made her choice and sold her sporty little car in order to pay off her student loans.

Veronica picked her way through the weeds and trash to the trailer's front door and knocked. As she suspected, there was no answer. The place was clearly uninhabitable. In fact, it appeared to be the last one standing on the abandoned lot. She looked across the street and was greeted with a sign of civilization—a convenience store in the midst of being remodeled.

The gas pump nozzles were covered with plastic bags. Half the store sported peeling paint underneath a sagging banner announcing they were open despite the mess. The other half had new beige siding, but it was rectangular, windowless, and drab.

Veronica got back in the car and turned off the useless GPS. She was a small-town girl now—she could do things the small-town way. She'd ask at the convenience store if anyone knew her grandfather or could offer directions.

She drove across the street, parked, and walked to the glass doors propped open by two cases of beer. She tugged her denim blazer around her and continued inside.

Dust swirled in the air. Behind the counter, a man held a gray-white panel against the open framework of an inside wall. His white T-shirt stretched tight across his back as he pounded nails into the panel.

Her skin tingled with excitement. Grandfather's offer was for her to work for his construction firm for thirty days before she took over running the distribution company he owned. And already she'd spotted an opportunity to take on a construction job. This man could hire her to remodel his store so he could focus on running his business. Windows, some pretty wooden-lattice trim on the outside, and white, lacy curtains inside would create an inviting ambiance.

She watched, trancelike, as the man's forearms flexed. If his biceps were any indication, he knew what he was doing with a hammer. Which, unfortunately, was more than she could say for herself. Luckily, she'd been studying her *Do-It-Yourself Home Improvement Manual*, so she wasn't completely clueless about what she was getting into.

"Can I help you?" Apparently at some point while she'd been ogling, he'd stopped pounding and turned toward her. His cinnamon-brown eyes locked on hers, and he hooked his hammer into the side of his tool belt.

Veronica never realized she had a weakness for a man in a tool belt. But wow, she'd have to be dead not to. She gulped and dragged her eyes back up to his attractively scruffy face, which added to the proof she was plenty weak but far from dead. "I hope so. I'm lost and in need of directions."

"To the interstate?"

"No, that I could find." She looked away from the golden flecks in the man's eyes and landed on his tough-guy chin just begging to be caressed. She had to focus. She was done being arm candy. "I'm looking for a man by the name of Ron Walker. I thought the address he gave me was for his house, but it led me to that trailer across the street."

The guy's grin was slow and lazy. "Ron definitely doesn't live there. In a few more weeks, that trailer will be gone, and the lot will be a baseball field."

"So you know Ron?" Veronica curled her toes inside her black, ankle-high boots, trying to ignore the awareness that fairly crackled around them and instead to concentrate on the helpful information he could provide. "This is great. I knew I was going to love small-town life."

"You're staying here?" He seemed surprised.

"Absolutely. I'm Veronica Jamison, Ron's granddaughter. He invited me to live with him." She smiled widely and held out her right hand, looking forward to the feel of his big workman's palm engulfing it in a shake.

"Matt Shaw." He took her hand but didn't hold it long, as if he didn't quite trust her. "What do you plan to do while you're here?"

"I'll be running his distribution warehouse eventually, but first I'm going to work for this construction company he has an investment in—Kortville Construction. I don't know if you've heard of it."

"Oh…I've heard of it." His voice sounded strangled.

"Are you okay?" Veronica took a step toward him.

"I'll call Ron and let him know you're here." Matt grabbed his cell phone off his tool belt and stalked out of the store.

· · ·

She misinterpreted my offer. Send her over, and I'll set her straight. Those were the words Matt imagined would come from Ron's mouth, accompanied by a big, hearty laugh.

Instead, Ron said, "No kidding! She *actually* came? I never thought she'd have the guts to defy her parents. I guess you'd better come over. I have some explaining to do."

Matt certainly *would* come to Ron's house. Kortville Construction only hired employees who'd proven they were capable of and willing to provide hard work. This bombshell blonde didn't have a single callus on her soft hands and was wearing fashion boots that would blister her feet before her lunch break.

Veronica sauntered out of the building toward him. She

looked from Matt to his truck with the Kortville Construction logo emblazoned on the door, and her mouth formed a tiny *O* of surprise. Apparently, she hadn't made the connection until now.

He searched for her car, but only a twenty-year-old Oldsmobile and Barney's rusted Blazer were in the lot. She must have had some driver drop her off. "If your guy already left, you can ride to Ron's with me."

"I'll follow you." She walked to the olive-colored Olds and got in.

Now Matt was surprised. His ex-girlfriend had taught him enough about expensive fashions that he could spot high class a mile away. This woman had high class—and high maintenance—written all over her. Yet, she was driving a car that was worth less than her high-heeled boots.

He made sure she stayed in his rearview mirror as he drove past his office and the diner. Then he signaled and turned left down Main Street. On one side was the bank and Laundromat with six washers and five quarter-eating dryers. The post office, hardware, and grocery stores all shared the same brick storefront on the other side of the street. Matt waved to Wilbur and Agatha Hollister, sitting on their usual bench out front, watching the cars go by. He chuckled, thinking of how they'd probably spend the rest of the afternoon debating the identity of the person driving the car behind him.

He turned again at the police and volunteer fire station, then drove past the library—which reminded him he'd forgotten to return Jenny's book; he knew if he didn't turn it in by tonight, Mrs. Parker would be stopping by his house to demand it in person.

When he stopped on the street in front of Ron's house, Veronica pulled around him into the driveway. They reached the front door at the same time.

"Thank you for your help." She smiled at him as she pushed the doorbell. "I can take it from here."

Matt didn't move. He wasn't leaving until Ron assured him he'd check out the references Veronica had provided for her previous construction work.

Ron opened the door, shuffling a little as he always did with his bad leg.

"Grandfather." Veronica glided toward him with her arms outstretched for a hug.

"Grandfather?" He looked shocked as he stood awkwardly in her embrace. "I was never a grandpa to you."

"But now that's all going to change." She beamed at Ron. "Thank you for bringing me here and giving me this opportunity. I can't wait to make up for lost time."

He cleared his throat, looking distinctly uncomfortable. "Why don't you just call me Ron?"

"Of-of course. That makes more sense until we get to know each other better." She dropped her arms and stepped back.

Matt wasn't a guy prone to hugging every stranger who came his way, but even he recoiled at Ron's cold reception. Ron had invited her here, yet his attitude clearly proclaimed he didn't want any of the things Veronica expected from her visit. Their lack of grandfather-granddaughter relationship wasn't Matt's problem, though—in fact, it proved that Ron had no intention of setting this woman up to work for Matt's company. He was home free. "If you're just having a family reunion, I'll leave you two alone. Nice to meet you, Veronica."

"She came here to work for you," Ron told him.

Matt gritted his teeth in frustration. "I'd like to check her references from her previous employer before we make a decision."

"She wants to work construction, and I want to hire my

granddaughter," Ron said. "So she's hired."

This was ridiculous. The woman had probably never held a hammer in her life. Matt, for one, had better things to do than teach her how.

Veronica turned and faced him. "I might not have done hands-on construction before, but I've been studying what you do. I can quickly put it to practical use."

Matt raised an eyebrow at Ron. Surely he would reconsider his foolish decision.

"Thirty days. That's all I'm asking," Ron said. "I've sat quietly by and let you run things the way you've seen fit. But I have a fifty percent ownership stake, and I'm exercising my voice. This is your new employee for the next month, unless she decides to return to her parents before then."

"Which I won't," Veronica asserted.

Right.

"She's proving herself to me," Ron explained. "Then I'll let her run my distribution warehouse out by the interstate."

And it was okay to use Matt's life as practice? He tried to rein in his anger. "I thought you were selling that and retiring."

"I *am* retiring. I'd planned to give it to my daughter before she ran off with that fancy city man. Now I have another chance to pass it down to my family instead of selling."

After he's promised a share of the sale's proceeds to every needy cause in town? Furious beyond the ability to speak rationally, Matt gritted out, "I'm going back to work."

Ron wouldn't renege on his promise to Kortville, because Veronica was never going to last the thirty days working for him. Matt knew her type, and he knew she wasn't cut out for small-town living *or* construction work. As long as Veronica Jamison was around him, she would have both—in spades.

• • •

"So, you'll work for him," Ron announced as Matt stalked to his truck.

Veronica watched him slam the door and spin his tires as he sped off. For the first time, she felt a sense of trepidation about the decision she'd made. "I don't think he's happy about it."

"He'll come around. I'll give you his number, so you can contact him to work out the details."

If only Grandfather—Ron, she corrected—had explained to Matt ahead of time that she was coming. She'd assumed the other owner of the construction company was agreeable to the decision to hire her, and a friendly welcome would have gone a long way toward calming her nerves. She punched Matt's number into her phone and then slipped it back in her purse. "Why don't I unpack and get settled? I'll talk to him after he's had a couple hours to get used to the idea."

"Brilliant plan." Ron gave a nod of approval and put his hand on the door, as if he was about to close it.

"Do you want to show me around before I bring in my suitcase, or is there another door that's closer to my room?"

"What? You're not staying here."

"I'm not?" He'd invited her to come for a month. She tried to remember the exact phrasing of the e-mail. Maybe he hadn't *explicitly* used the words *stay in my house*, but they'd certainly been implied…

"Absolutely not." He seemed extremely uncomfortable by the notion. "I'm an old man; I've lived alone for nearly thirty years. I have one bathroom in this house, and I don't want any of your frivolous lotions cluttering it up."

"I'll be careful not to leave anything behind." Her grandfather had appeared much more welcoming when she'd first e-mailed him for advice about leaving her parents' home—he'd immediately offered her a job and a place to stay. Maybe he wasn't as open when it came to face-to-face meetings, but with a little time, she knew she could get him to warm up, and then they could make up for all the years they'd never had together.

"I don't want you in there at all. I'm seventy-eight years old. When I have to go, I have to go. If you'd followed my directions to the trailer, you'd know you already have a place. You can stay there for as long as you're in town."

"That trailer? You mean the address wasn't a mistake?"

"Of course not." He sounded offended. "My body might be falling apart, but there's nothing wrong with my mind."

Panic fluttered in her stomach. She'd been prepared to make sacrifices, like sharing a bathroom. But moving into the only home in a run-down, practically condemned trailer park sounded downright dangerous. "I…I'd really rather stay with you."

"I went out of my way to provide you with this very generous offer. You can take it or leave it," Ron told her.

Veronica squared her shoulders. She knew she couldn't spend her entire life living with family. She was an adult, after all, and if she wanted to be treated like one, she needed to live like one. "D-do you have a key for me?"

"The door should be unlocked," Ron said.

She didn't know whether this detail was supposed to relax her or frighten her, so she tried to joke. "Unlocked as in 'housekeeping is tidying up for my arrival' or unlocked as in 'enter the local thugs' hangout at my own risk'?"

Ron didn't crack a smile. "I have nothing in there worth stealing. If you're looking for maid service, you'd better go back to your parents and all the wonderful things they're willing to give you."

Sure, she could have all that money could offer. All she had to do was give up her chance to build the career she'd fought so hard to begin.

No big deal.

The trailer door stuck so badly she couldn't even turn the handle. As if that wasn't frustrating enough, the knob was sticky. With what, Veronica didn't want to speculate.

She suspected Matt hadn't cooled down to the point where he'd gladly lend a hand. She decided to leave him alone, to give him time to warm up to the idea of working closely with her.

The perfect solution was right in front of her: she'd fix the doorknob. It would prove to Matt that she had skills and that she wouldn't burden his company, and it would show her grandfather she appreciated his generosity and intended to persevere despite the obstacles.

She removed the thick hardcover *Do-It-Yourself Home Improvement Manual* from the trunk of her car and found the section that talked about doorknobs. She moved her finger down the page. *Troubleshooting.*

Cylinders could be frozen. She lifted her face to the sun. The day was nearly sixty degrees, a beautiful start to the month of May. Ice shouldn't be a problem.

Obstructed or damaged keyway. She looked from the book back to the trailer entrance. No, the door was supposed to be unlocked already.

Many lock and doorknob problems can be solved by cleaning and lubricating the bolt mechanism. A-ha! She slapped the book closed and walked across the street for some disinfecting wipes and oil.

Veronica stepped into the store and glanced around. There were aisles of prepackaged snacks and a wall of refrigerated beverages, but she didn't see any cleaning supplies. She headed for the counter, where Matt was no longer pounding his nails on the wall, to ask for assistance. In Matt's place was a potbellied man, wiping dust off boxes of cigarettes with a bored expression. He didn't look up when he said, "What's your brand? Pack or carton?"

"Barney, she's not here for cigarettes. She's Veronica Jamison," Matt said as he entered the store, carrying a huge bucket that read ALL-PURPOSE JOINT COMPOUND. She had no idea what that was, although the bucket looked heavy. She'd have to research it in her book.

The clerk's head snapped up, and his eyes narrowed. He didn't look bored anymore, but he didn't exactly appear friendly, either. "So you're moving into the trailer park? Let me get you a box of doughnuts as a welcome present."

"Actually, I need disinfecting wipes and lubricating oil."

"The doughnuts are a better deal." He waddled over to a dust-covered tray, picked up an equally dusty empty box, and began filling it with what might have once been chocolate doughnuts but were now merely gray-white lumps of construction dust.

She attempted to keep her expression politely neutral. "That's very nice of you, but I really do need some cleaning supplies…"

"Nonsense. You're malnourished. You need doughnuts." He dumped the entire tray into the box.

A white cloud puffed between them. Veronica tried to convince herself it was only powdered sugar, except she didn't think any of the doughnuts had a powdered-sugar coating, at least not to start with. Matt stood behind Barney, silently laughing so hard that he was unable to work.

Veronica tried once again to gracefully extricate herself from this situation. "Actually, I'm on a budget, and I didn't factor doughnuts into it…"

"On the house." Barney plopped the box into her hands, slung his arm around her, and propelled her to the door.

She tried to dig her heels in and turn down an aisle, but before she could change direction, she found herself on the sidewalk outside. "Thank you, but I still need—"

"Not on that budget you don't." He removed his heavy arm from her shoulders and lifted the case of beer out of the open doorway. With a smirk that convinced her his actions had been calculated to shut her out, he then stepped inside with the beer, letting the door close behind him. He hadn't exactly let it hit her on the butt on her way out, but he might as well have.

Small-town hospitality was…interesting.

A moment later, Matt came through the door and headed for his truck again.

She followed him. "Does Barney do that to everyone?"

He glanced from her to her dusty gift and smirked. "Just the gold diggers."

The reminder of Ron's cold reception smarted. "I'm not gold digging for anything. I'm going to work for every penny."

"In those clothes?" Matt's tone was derisive.

"Look, just because I have nice clothes doesn't mean I can't work hard." She was wearing jeans, a denim jacket, work boots, and a cute pink bandana holding back her blond hair.

She'd dressed for construction.

• • •

Matt didn't bother answering; he simply refilled his nail pouch. He could use every one, and it wouldn't be enough to pound out his frustrations.

Veronica set her toxic welcome gift on the tailgate of

his truck. "I can see you're not crazy about my coming down here, not knowing you or your company and working for you. But I've been studying up on construction. I think you'll be surprised by how much I already know. I won't slow you down."

Matt turned away from his supplies to stare at her. If she was as sincere as she sounded, then she was even more naive than he'd been when he assumed he'd have Ron's investment paid back quickly, regardless of the financial mess his brother had left for him, a tanking economy, and an imploding housing market that had given him no other option but to take Ron's bailout offer. "If you say so."

"I do," Veronica replied firmly. She reached into the bucket and pulled out a single nail. "I'm ready to prove it. Do you have an extra hammer?"

"What would you pound that nail into if I gave you one?" He walked around her and slid a panel of Sheetrock out of the back of the truck.

"Into this thing, I assume." She reached for the other end of the drywall with the hand that wasn't holding the nail. Her one-handed approach threw off the precarious balance of the long, wide, flat slab. One corner dipped to the ground and crumpled against the pavement.

Matt sighed, calculating it would take at least two rounds of joint compound to smooth it into shape. He needed to convince this woman to go back to her spoiled party-girl life while a small patching job was the worst problem she caused. "Around here, pounding a couple nails doesn't count as a full day of work. Now, I have a job to do. If you're not going to leave town, you can unpack, and I'll talk to you in the morning."

She cleared her throat. "That was my plan. But the door's stuck, and I can't get into the trailer."

Luckily, the Sheetrock was still resting on the ground, or he would have dropped it in shock. "You're staying in the trailer? The one across the street?"

A funny little smile softened the determination on her face. "If I can get the door open. I think the knob needs some oil, but apparently I can only get doughnuts on my welcome visit to this store."

"I'll help you." Matt rubbed his chest and smiled. Veronica Jamison would be headed home today after all, as soon as she got a good look at her living quarters. He was more than happy to give her a guided tour.

Matt held the outer screen and tried to turn the knob on the front door. It didn't budge.

She put her hand on the screen, holding it away from him. "What about that oil for the bolt mechanism?"

"It just needs a little muscle." He turned the knob as hard as he could, shoving his body against the door. The wood trembled, but the knob didn't even wiggle.

"Do you think Ron would have locked it?"

"It's not locked." He'd never known Ron to lock a door— either for his house or his car. In this case, anyone who stole from the trailer would have done Ron a favor. Matt slammed his shoulder against the wood again, and the door splintered open. He stumbled through the suddenly open space, bumping against a dusty brown chair and falling to his knees on the sticky linoleum.

"Oh my gosh. Are you okay?" Veronica stood over him, looking down with concern and something he was fairly certain was rich-girl condescension.

"Fine." His shoulder throbbed mercilessly, and he felt like

an idiot.

"Oh, good." She started giggling and then full out laughing.

"What?" A nerve twitched behind his eye. He might not be able to control if she worked for him, but he certainly wouldn't put up with her laughing at him.

"You're lying on the door." He realized her laughter was full of genuine mirth, not a drop of malice.

Still lying on the floor, Matt looked around to orient himself and realized she was right. He'd ripped the door, hinges and all, straight off the rotting frame. The only thing missing was the doorknob. When he located it still in the frame, still hanging out of the open doorway where the door had been, he started to laugh, too. This woman had to believe he was the biggest hick who ever lived, by destroying doors instead of doing the sensible thing and taking the lock apart.

Veronica reached out her hand to help him up. He accepted it, but they were both laughing too hard to manage an effective effort to get him on his feet and she dropped down next to him. He released her hand and took a deep breath. He couldn't remember the last time he'd laughed until he was too weak to stand.

"I can't believe you busted the door out of its frame!" she said.

"I can't believe you just used the word *busted*." He laughed harder at hearing it come out of her high-class mouth. He looked over at her sitting next to him on the broken door and shook his head at the absolute ridiculousness of the situation, a situation he was *enjoying*. He pulled himself together to stand and then offered his hand to Veronica.

She accepted, still laughing as he hauled her up. As he pushed open the screen and tossed the door out of the trailer onto the lawn, Veronica stepped to the door frame and fiddled with the lock. The knob still didn't turn, so she pulled it straight out from the wall.

Well, dang. Who would have thought she knew what a bolt mechanism was? Let alone that it was the broken piece that had kept the door from opening?

"Let's see if anything else needs a little lubrication that you can destroy for me," she teased, as she set the knob on the gray countertop of the kitchen.

Like any other red-blooded man, the word *lubrication* triggered immediate fantasies. Matt stared at the duct-taped window, mentally drawing up an estimate of labor and materials until he had his body under control. When he was settled, he glanced at Veronica to gauge if she'd been purposely pushing his buttons.

She flicked a smile at him, still seemingly focused on the innocent moment they'd shared over the broken door.

Whether she had brains under her gorgeous head of silky blond hair was debatable. But he clearly did not. He hadn't learned from his mistakes. He was still pretty much a sucker for rich girls and their smiles.

He needed to refocus on the reason he'd offered to help her get inside the trailer in the first place. "You'll pay as much to replace that window as the whole trailer's worth. The counters were originally white, you know. This chair used to be tan, and so was the floor."

"Well then, when I'm not hammering, I guess I'll be cleaning," Veronica said over her shoulder as she sashayed to the back of the trailer.

So, she was going to make him work for it? He was up to the challenge.

His heavy boots stuck with each step on the gray-brown floor as he followed her. But then he stopped in the doorway. A big bed filled the entire room. He didn't dare come any closer.

"I'm not going to ask how anyone could get a mattress that size in here," she commented.

He kept his expression neutral. "I expect rodents have turned it into a warm, cozy nest."

She shivered, as he intended, but didn't scream. "I'll definitely have to do a mouse check if I'm going to sleep here. Maybe I could use those doughnuts from Barney as bait to lure them out."

Nice comeback. His respect increased another notch. "My guess is you'd end up with mice from all the vacant lots over here, too."

She turned away from the bed to him, and Matt found himself staring into her clear blue eyes. "If the mice start chasing me, I *will* knock you down to get out of here. You know that, right? Your shoulder ramming trick is a really great technique."

He snorted. Sure it was, if one didn't particularly care whether he regained full use of his shoulder or not. Matt rolled it against the dull ache and rotated his neck as he stepped out of the door frame, where he'd been inadvertently blocking her in.

Veronica walked by him into the bathroom and ran the water in the shower and sink. The basins wouldn't win any awards for cleanliness, but for a building on the verge of demolition, the pipes surprisingly appeared to be in working order.

Her shoulder brushed his as she continued to the kitchen. Matt stepped back, irritated that he'd allowed himself to gravitate so close to her trim, energetic body. He was raising a kid and was intent on spending the rest of his life in this town—both deal breakers for rich city girls.

She opened the refrigerator and immediately slammed

it shut. The rancid, moldy smell hit him a second later. Now *there* was a reminder to stay as far back as possible.

Veronica patted her hand against the refrigerator. "Would you mind throwing this outside with the front door?"

Her sense of humor about the entire trailer threw him off. She was supposed to be leaving him in a cloud of dust by now. He needed to cut the camaraderie and get tough with her before he ended up saddled with her on a job site. "You're not seriously thinking of living here. It's uninhabitable."

"Are you offering me accommodations?"

He crossed his arms over his chest. He didn't want her staying in this trailer—no one should have to live in these conditions. But even if he didn't have an impressionable niece under his roof, he couldn't make the mistake of pretending he had anything to offer someone like her. She must have options. Girls like her always did. She just needed to use them.

"That's what I thought." She pushed open the screen and walked out of the trailer.

Matt followed, wishing he could crack a joke about being careful not to run over any mice as she drove off. But he'd pushed her away just as he'd intended, and he worried his comment would come across as purposely rude.

He pulled the flimsy screen door tight behind him and shoved the front door out of the walkway into the tiny patch of overgrown weeds that passed for the trailer's yard. He looked up, prepared to send her off with a friendly wave.

But instead of backing out of the driveway, Veronica was tugging her designer suitcase from her trunk.

He ran over and grabbed the expensive luggage with one hand, lifting it onto the gravel next to the car. "Why are you driving this piece of junk anyway?"

"It's my car now." She put her hand next to his on the suitcase.

Heat traveled up his arm, but he ignored it. "You had a different car—a nice one—before this." It wasn't a question. A girl like her shouldn't be caught dead riding in this car, let alone driving it without roadside assistance on standby.

She moved her hand away, straightened, and looked him in the eye. "Yes, I had a nice car and a nice house. I'm very aware that I traded down quite a few notches below my comfort level. But that doesn't make me a snob. It doesn't mean I won't be a good construction worker."

"It doesn't mean you *will* be a good construction worker, either," he pointed out.

Her lips compressed into a determined line. "I'm not a fluffy airhead who runs screaming from a little refrigerator odor. I'm going to work beside you for the full thirty days. If that means making you miserable because you're in the middle of what I have to do to make a future for myself, I'm sorry. But I can't change my life to make you happy. I'm doing what I need to make my *own* life."

Kimberly had told him the same thing when she'd left. She hadn't cared if she broke his heart and made his life miserable. No way was she staying in this dinky town to help him pick up the pieces of his brother's life and raise his orphaned niece. She had a life to live, and no one was getting in her way.

At least this time Matt knew exactly the type of woman he was dealing with. And his heart would be completely safe.

Chapter Two

Veronica clutched the two dull silver keys in her hand. One was to a car so ancient it belonged in a trash heap or a museum. The other was for a door that was sprawled over a third of her lawn. Yes, she'd given up her fun convertible and suite in her parents' house to get them. But more importantly, she'd gotten them through her own efforts and contacts.

For the first time in her twenty-seven years, she was living completely alone, not in the halfway independence of college dorms or sorority houses. She'd taken her first steps toward creating her own life, and she'd made significant progress for the first day. Unfortunately, if she wanted to make it to day two, she needed to scour and sanitize the trailer until she could sit, lie on, and touch the furnishings.

The common-sense approach would be to call a maid service. But she was without her credit, debit, ATM cards, or checking account. Her cash was meager and needed to be rationed carefully if she had any hope of making it through her first construction paycheck.

She'd have to clean the place. Which meant she needed disinfecting wipes and bleach—things the convenience store clerk would likely hide behind the counter while he plied her with toxic food. That was his loss, then.

She turned the key in her car and listened to the engine grind and sputter. She didn't have a clue what she'd do if the car didn't start, but thankfully it eventually came to life—just as her cell phone rang from inside her purse. "Hello?"

"Darling, I've been so worried about you. You never called to tell me you made the trip safely. Has your grandfather been horrible?"

She deserved this for not checking the display before she answered. "Hello, Mother. Sorry I didn't call when I got down here. I assumed when you said I was cut out of your life, you meant it."

"Well, yes, I did. We still do." She didn't sound certain. "Your father and I are very disappointed with your choices lately. But to not call and tell us you arrived safely caused us unnecessary worry. We tried to track you down through your Porsche. You can imagine our shock when we found out you sold your graduation present."

Veronica pinched the bridge of her nose. "I didn't want a graduation present. I wanted my résumé to be taken seriously."

"Don't get in a snit. You've been raised to be a wonderful society wife."

Mother had to understand this was much more than a snit. This was her standing up for what she wanted for her future. "I got my business degree so I could take over the family company, which I would have been groomed for my whole life if I'd been a son. When Dad wouldn't give me a job because I *only* had a bachelor's degree, I went back and got my MBA at my *own* expense. Now he won't hire me and he's warned everyone in the trade association not to, either, because I have too much education and no work experience to go with it. I've been begging for work experience since I was eighteen."

"Darling, do we have to rehash this argument?"

She sighed and put the car in gear. "No, we don't, Mother." It wouldn't do her any good. Her parents refused to listen. They only considered what they thought was best for her and what they thought she wanted, no matter how many times she tried to explain differently.

"Good, I'm so glad it's settled. Trevor will be over the moon. His assistant tells me he's heartsick for you to come home and marry him. We have a VIP table at the Help the Less Fortunate fund-raiser tomorrow. It's the perfect place to announce your engagement."

"I'm not coming home, Mother, and I'm not marrying Trevor." She pulled the phone away from her ear and deliberately clicked it off. The only thing Trevor Tyler Cunningham IV was heartsick about was losing his chance to get his hands on her father's company. He couldn't have cared less about her being part of the package deal.

She rattled her way through town until she located the tiny strip of storefronts that she'd driven by when she'd followed Matt earlier. An elderly couple still sat in the exact same spot in front of the grocery store. They gaped at her as she stepped out of the car.

"Good afternoon," she called, determined to do her part to promote small-town friendliness, as well as not let the call from her mother ruin her mood.

The man squinted at her. He had a thin white mustache and thinner white hair and was wearing red plaid pants with a green striped shirt. "You must be the prodigal granddaughter everyone's talking about."

Prodigal made it sound as if she'd run away and returned; it sounded accusatory. She couldn't even imagine what interest they would have in someone they'd never met and had no connection to. "Must have been a short conversation. I haven't been here long enough to give anyone anything to say."

"That's not what I hear," he retorted.

The woman was wearing a dress printed with giant orange and fuchsia flowers, her gray hair pulled back in a tight bun. She elbowed him. "That's enough, Wilbur. Give the girl time to get her bearings before you lay into her."

"Give her time to destroy all our plans to improve this town, you mean. Well, I'm not giving up my dream of starting a food pantry and community closet." He pushed his palms on his red plaid knees, stood shakily, and shuffled away.

"I'm not here to destroy anything, especially a food pantry," Veronica told the woman, baffled and hurt by the accusations. "I love charity work. If there's something I can do to help out, please tell me."

The woman glanced at the man walking away, and then back to Veronica. "I'll talk to him. He's not going to roll over easily, but then again, neither should you." She stood and followed the old man down the sidewalk.

Veronica swallowed her question of what she might have to fight for as the couple disappeared into the Laundromat. She already knew the answer was everything. She'd spent too much of her life giving other people what they wanted, and now she needed to do something for herself.

She stepped purposefully into the grocery store and loaded her cart with cleaning supplies, bypassing the food. There was no point in trying to stock her cabinets or refrigerator; anything inside them wasn't making its way into her mouth. She wasn't sure if the refrigerator was salvageable, regardless of how much she sanitized it.

She set her bottles and sponges on the checkout belt.

The cashier, whose name tag said "Becca", glared at her. "The credit card machine's broken, and we don't take out-of-town checks."

"That's all right. I have cash." Veronica forced a smile. This woman knew exactly who she was. Her reputation was preceding her, and it definitely wasn't a good thing.

Becca lifted the first item off the conveyor. "Mayor Wilbur and Agatha Hollister sit on that bench all day. Nobody's ever driven them away before. Whatever you said must have been downright rude and awful."

Good grief, the *mayor* was out to get her. Was it possible that Trevor's connections extended this far across the state? "I certainly didn't mean to be. If I gave them a bad impression, I'll talk to them and try to correct it."

Becca's fingers paused over the register keys. "Do us all a favor—don't. Leave our residents alone. Leave Ron's plans alone. And for goodness sake, let Matt run his company without babysitting you while he's doing it."

Veronica clenched her purse strap as frustration coursed through her. Women had powerful careers across the country, including at her father's company. Yet, wherever she attempted to start hers, she was patted on the head and shuffled to the corporate equivalent of the daycare room.

The cashier jabbed her finger on the register keypad. "You owe forty-two twenty-five."

The final dollar amount took Veronica's mind off her never-ending career battle. Cleaning supplies added up quickly. She was going to have to watch her budget. She took a fifty from her wallet and handed it to the clerk.

Becca gave her a long look before she took the bill. She turned it over in her hand and held it to the light. Then she picked up the intercom microphone next to the register. "Manager to the front to verify possible fraudulent currency."

"Fraudulent?" Veronica glanced around for a fraudster lurking in the corner.

"It's got goofy colors on it," she drawled. "I can't let you city people try to pass off your fake currency on us unsuspecting small-town folks."

Veronica had never heard anything so ridiculous. She was a step away from being accused of a federal offense. Were her father and Trevor trying to frame her in order to convince her to come home, or was the town simply out to get her? "A bank employee handed it to me this morning. It's been in my possession ever since."

The manager walked over, glanced at the empty bench outside, and exchanged a meaningful look with Becca. Then he took the crisp bill and examined it more thoroughly. Veronica shifted her feet. More employees, along with customers, gathered around the register, each taking their turn to handle and inspect the money.

People filtered in through the front door to add to the crowd. She'd left fifty-dollar bills as tips before; now there was a line to look at one. A man in a sport coat and tie and another man in a police uniform worked their way to the front of the crowd. Veronica stared at the uniformed officer and then back at the store manager.

"You called the *cops*? This is absurd." Her instinct was to open her cell phone and call her lawyer, but the lawyer was a friend of her father's and therefore off-limits.

"It's colorful. Money in this country's supposed to be green," Becca rationalized, her eyes round and innocent.

The cop smirked.

"We don't get many fifties here." The store manager managed to keep a straight face as he passed the bill to the balding man in the suit. "We want to be extra-cautious. We were fortunate that our bank president was available to stop in for a look."

"You called the president of the bank?" Veronica couldn't believe it. If the mayor or Matt had paid with a fifty, she bet no one would have batted an eye.

The banker took his spectacles out of the inside breast pocket of his suit coat and perched them on his nose as he inspected the bill. When he was done, he removed his glasses, folded them with agonizing slowness, and placed them back in his pocket. He smoothed his tie and handed the bill to the manager. "Unfortunately, it's legitimate. It has all the security features embedded. Fifties are now made with multiple colors, just like the newer twenties, tens, and fives."

All of which have been around for years now, Veronica resisted pointing out. She would accept their apology graciously. Perhaps someone in the crowd would become her first friend in town.

"Better safe than sorry," the manager muttered. "Thanks for trying, Becca."

There was a murmur of agreement as the gathering slowly dispersed. Veronica continued to stand at the register, her neck aching from holding her head so straight. As far as she could tell, her father and Trevor weren't behind this. Which meant she was hated just because Ron had dared to invite her here.

Well, the witch hunt wasn't going to drive her away. She had too much at stake to leave because of someone else's opinion. Ron hadn't exactly welcomed her into his house, but he'd shown his willingness to give her a chance by lining up a job for her. Everyone else could at least give her the benefit of the doubt that her currency was genuine.

"You're done," Becca said. "You proved your point. You paid. You can go."

"I have seven seventy-five in change coming." She

wouldn't be humiliated into leaving without it—she'd done nothing wrong. She wouldn't let these people treat her like a criminal. She definitely wasn't *that* kind of person.

Dollar bills clutched in her hand, she marched back outside and settled into her ancient green tank. She turned the key, checked the mirrors to back up, and discovered the flashing lights of a squad car blocking her in.

Tears pressed against her eyelids. She blinked them back as she rolled down her window for the approaching officer with the name badge "Connor O'Malley," the same man who'd been inside watching the checkout drama with amusement only minutes ago. "What is the problem, sir?"

"This vehicle has a broken taillight. License, registration, and insurance, please."

"What?" She was sure when she'd bought it this morning all the lights and signals had been in working order.

"Yep. And since you were going to drive away and leave the broken pieces on the ground, I'll have to write you up for littering, as well." Officer O'Malley was practically gleeful.

"Are you saying someone smashed my taillight, and instead of trying to find the culprit and arrest him or her, you're giving me a ticket?"

"I can also write you up for disturbing the peace and verbally abusing an officer."

She resisted laying her head on the steering wheel; she had to work on creating some goodwill. She understood Matt's distrust and resentment—he was her employer and hadn't been consulted about her hiring. But the townspeople had taken up his cause without knowing the first thing about her.

Unless she wanted to crawl back under her parents' thumbs and live a luxurious, empty life as Mrs. Trevor Tyler Cunningham IV, she had to prove to these people that she deserved a chance. Her dreams and career plans should matter as much as everyone else's.

Her head felt like it was full of concrete. Veronica didn't try to lift it off the pillow as she took in the sounds from outside. Birds chirped incessantly. A single car drove by, close enough she could hear the crunch of rocks under the tires and the slam of a door. Someone shouted, followed shortly by an answering bark from a dog. Light pricked her eyelids.

She'd just closed her eyes. It couldn't possibly be morning already.

Considering how long it had taken her to make the bedroom and bathroom habitable enough to wash her face and go to sleep, she probably *had* closed her eyes only minutes ago. Despite the gaping hole in the screen, she'd left the window wide open last night. With all the cleaning chemicals she'd gone through, she was afraid of asphyxiating herself if she didn't let the place air out. She started to fumble for her cell phone to check the time, but then voices across the street carried inside.

"Rich girl didn't show up, huh?" a man asked, the same voice that had called for the dog a few minutes ago.

"Yeah, looks like that baseball field will get finished right on schedule after all." That was Matt's deep, rumbling tone. Funny how she could recognize it after only a couple short conversations.

She squinted against the blinding light. The trailer had no curtains or shades, and the sun shone straight across her pillow.

"You're going to write her off because she's a few minutes late?" a woman countered.

"If I can get my work done instead of participating in some *Debutante Checking Out How the Other Ninety-Nine Percent Lives* reality TV show, believe me, I'm going to jump on it," Matt replied.

Veronica rolled off the bed that she'd carefully inspected and determined to be rodent-free, despite Matt's dire warnings. She grabbed a new pair of jeans from her suitcase and pushed her legs into them. Her real life was at stake, not any reality show.

She had to prove herself as his equal and worthy of his respect. She wouldn't let him brush her off like her father had, like Matt had yesterday when she'd tried to help with the convenience-store job. After today, she would only have twenty-nine more days before she took over the distribution center from her grandfather—a business she was well qualified to run.

"Give her a call on her cell phone, and leave it up to her to decide if she wants to come," the woman said. "Then you'll be off the hook with Ron when he finds out."

Veronica kept her body below the window ledge as she changed her shirt, and then peeked out as she snapped her jeans. Barney was standing in the entrance to the convenience store, holding a big black dog by the collar. The woman from the bench yesterday—Agatha Hollister, dressed in lavender pants and an olive-green starched blouse that looked like it was cut from someone's front curtains—was talking with Matt.

Veronica wasn't sure if Agatha was defending her or making sure Matt didn't get himself in trouble. The former would have been a nice thought, but the people in the grocery store had trampled on her rose-colored glasses, so she had to assume the latter.

"I know better than to call her type at seven in the

morning," Matt said. "That's the equivalent of two or three in the morning to you and me."

It was only seven a.m.? No wonder she was exhausted. Much too tired to take issue with the disdain Matt used when he talked about "her type." Veronica's boots zipped along the side, so they were easy to put on. She brushed her teeth, combed her hair, and slid on lipstick.

When she came out of the bathroom, Agatha was still lecturing Matt on the courtesy of giving someone a phone call. If she'd thought there was a chance anyone in town might have a soft spot for her, she would have guessed the elderly woman was purposely stalling to give Veronica time to get her act together.

"I don't give wakeup calls to any of my employees," Matt said. "They take responsibility for themselves, and they pull their weight around the job site."

Veronica grabbed her denim blazer and her home-improvement manual, fumbled with the flimsy lock on the screen door, and slammed outside. "Give me a chance to prove myself before you decide whether or not I can pull my weight."

She couldn't tell whether Matt looked surprised or annoyed as she power walked across the road toward him. "It's after seven. You're late," he said.

"A start time was never specified." She didn't expect him to drop his condescension immediately, but she wasn't going to stop reminding him until he treated her as an equal. "Good morning, Barney. What a sweet pooch you have." She let his dog sniff her hand and then scratched it behind the ears. "Do you need help covering the doughnuts this morning so they don't get dusty?"

Barney turned his dog away from her and tramped inside the convenience store with it, letting the door slam shut behind them.

She tried again. "Good morning, Agatha. Do you have a pen and paper? I have a web address for you and your husband that has some great step-by-step information on starting a food pantry."

"Wilbur would love that." Agatha opened her purse and began shuffling through the contents.

Veronica turned her smile on Matt. At last, she was making progress. "I'm here. Are the drywall and nails in the back of your truck?" She was proud of figuring out the name of those gray-white slabs they'd been wrestling with yesterday.

He didn't look impressed. "I'm not working here this morning. Barney's still pretty ticked about me dusting up his fresh doughnuts yesterday. His sales were way down, and he had a lot of complaints."

"Imagine that," she murmured. Right now she was willing to blow her entire budget on a breakfast that would counteract the effect of too many cleaning chemicals, too little sleep, and an empty stomach. Too bad she'd run out of the trailer so fast she'd forgotten her purse. Barney's complimentary welcome gifts weren't exactly fit for consumption.

"I'm going to fix a gate," Matt said. "Are you coming or going back to bed?"

If he hadn't been so snotty about it, she'd much prefer to go back to bed. But she didn't have that luxury. She didn't want that luxury, she reminded herself. She wanted to work hard to make it on her own. "That's great. There's a whole chapter in my book about gates and fences. I am all over this job. Let me get my car, and I'll follow you."

Matt folded his arms over his chest, clearly not buying into the excitement she was attempting to generate. "You think reading a do-it-yourself article qualifies you to do construction work?"

"Not alone for my first job," she backpedaled, trying not to get distracted by his biceps bulging out from under his T-shirt sleeves. Appearances weren't everything, she reminded herself, and Matt hadn't exactly done much to show he had a personality worthy of his hot body. "That's why I'm working with you. My point was that you don't have to worry about getting me up to speed or my slowing you down or bothering you with simple questions."

"That's a relief," he said sarcastically.

All right. That was enough. "You don't know enough about me to have any clue what kind of qualifications I have. But I'll tell you what you *should* have figured out from the beginning. I am a human being with feelings, hopes, and dreams, just like you. Stop lobbing insults at me and treat me with respect."

"Amen," Agatha said, her severe gray bun bobbling with gusto. "I found a pen, so you can give me the name of that website."

Veronica blinked. She'd gotten so wrapped up in Matt she'd completely forgotten they had an audience. She took the pen and paper from Agatha and wrote down the information.

Matt stalked to the driver's side of his truck. "If you want to come, get in."

"Go with him," Agatha advised under her breath. "The more time you spend together, the more you'll learn."

Matt gunned the engine, and Veronica shot a grateful smile to Agatha before opening the passenger door. She needed space to pull herself together and become as impassive as he was. But she knew the old woman was right—she had to take every opportunity she could to learn about this business she was working for. Matt wasn't going to freely offer it to her.

More important than learning the ins and outs of the construction business was the fact that she needed the paycheck. She had more to clean and repair than she had money in her wallet. She'd sold everything of value to pay off the student loans from her business degree—the one that was supposed to make people take her seriously.

Veronica shivered. Nobody did, and she'd given up everything she could fall back on. Now she had to prove she was strong enough to do manual labor and work at the poverty line. Before she could prove it to Matt, her grandfather, and her parents, she had to prove it to herself.

• • •

"So you mend fences and remodel convenience stores. What else do you do?"

"A little bit of everything." Matt gulped his morning coffee and focused on the road. He didn't want to start a conversation. He'd already discovered yesterday afternoon that Veronica was charming and witty. It would be too easy to enjoy her company and want to impress her. The entire scenario would end with him falling far short of her expectations.

"You're a handyman." Veronica's tone implied the designation fell below construction worker on the social scale. She flipped open her book to a section titled *Fences, Posts, and Gates.*

"Yeah, pretty much." It wasn't the complete truth. He did plenty of handyman jobs, but he also ran a full-service construction firm. He enjoyed taking on big jobs, as long as he could preserve the reputation his brother had built for small-town personal service and keep himself on the front lines of the labor force. No amount of money was worth chaining himself to a desk, buried in paperwork. But there was no use explaining that to someone with her pedigree.

"How long will this job take?"

"About an hour." Probably longer with her distracting his focus and standing in his way. "Then I'll go back to the convenience store." He swerved around the massive pothole on the right side of the street, then turned into a driveway.

Veronica braced her hand on the dash and looked out the side window at the bumpy road. "Is that hole another project on the day's agenda?"

"Construction companies from bigger towns come in to do road projects." He bounced up the driveway and stopped at his favorite house in the whole county. It was an old-style farmhouse with peeling paint, old-fashioned shutters, and a drooping wraparound porch. Some day he was going to turn it into a beauty.

"Oh my gosh. This place is gorgeous. If you painted the house white and the shutters bright blue, it would look amazing. Oh, and you could put some big antique rocking chairs on the porch once you fix that up. Wow," she said, looking on in awe, "there is amazing potential here. What are we starting with?"

"The gate," he reminded her. He got out of the truck and walked around to open the tailgate, unsettled that she was so in tune with the way he coveted replacing those rotting floorboards, restoring the whole house and making it beautiful.

Veronica met him at the back of the truck. He grudgingly gave her points for not sitting in the vehicle waiting for him to open the passenger door. "Right. The gate." She shot another wistful look across the yard. "Is fixing up the rest of the house too big a project for your company, too?"

The insinuation smarted, although moments ago he'd wanted her to think his business was nothing short of pathetic. "Too much for the owner. Mrs. Parker's doing as much as she can afford right now."

Speaking of Mrs. Parker, he'd forgotten to return that darn library book again. He wasn't even sure where it was in his house. "When she's ready, she'll give me the green light to fix up the porch and paint the place." He liked the idea of blue shutters even better than his original plan for brown.

"And you're making a living off this business?" Veronica looked incredulous.

"Enough for me." Not enough to pay back Ron and regain complete ownership of his company. Not nearly enough to satisfy a high-class woman.

But Veronica was still focused on the building. "Wow. She must really love this house to live here in the condition it's in now."

"She hates it," Matt muttered. Knowing that made him want to fix it up even more and give it the love it deserved. He pulled out his tool belt, hammer, and some two-by-fours to use as temporary braces. "Grab two L brackets."

Veronica reluctantly looked away from the building, but she didn't glance at the materials in the truck. Instead, she opened her book to the index in the back. "There's nothing in here by that name. What are L brackets?"

"Steel angle. They look like the letter *L*."

"Wait, maybe they are in here." She flipped the pages and squinted at a picture. "Are they the same as butt joints or angle irons?" She looked up at him and grinned. "*Butt joints*, really? I'm pretty sure I have two butt joints, but I'm not going to build a gate with them."

He laughed, despite her having no intuition about construction at all. "You don't need to know every vocabulary word to know how to do it."

"Listen to this." She had her head buried in the book again. "'Resquare a sagging gate with a turnbuckle and wire.' Is that what you were going to do? Is a turnbuckle the same as the L-thingy?"

Still grinning with amusement, Matt ignored the question and grabbed the supplies he wanted. He didn't need to explain the process — she was never going to fix a gate in her life. She'd hit her limit within a few minutes or hours, and he could go back to getting his work done in peace. Unfortunately, working without her humor, sunny disposition, and wide, hopeful gaze didn't hold nearly as much appeal as it had yesterday.

Although the day was early, the weather was unusually warm. Matt shoved a baseball hat on his head to give himself a bit of shade. Veronica sauntered around the truck in her skinny jeans, fussing with her pink bandana.

He walked ahead of her so he wouldn't act on the sudden and bizarre urge to slide his fingers through her hair. By the time she joined him, he'd removed the lopsided wooden gate from its hinges.

"Prop this up somewhere." He held the bulky structure out to her, but she had her book under her arm and was still messing with the silly bandana. Instead of dropping everything to take it, she brushed her toe over the deep gouge in the earth that the gate's lopsidedness had created. "What caused it to sag this much?"

He set the gate out of the way himself. "You can look it up in your book later; the cause doesn't matter. You need to pay attention to how to fix it right so it doesn't start sagging again tomorrow. Lean against this post to push it back in position, and then I'll secure it."

"The solution would make more sense if I understood the cause," Veronica murmured, but she leaned against the post like he'd instructed.

Matt pounded the braces in place, his hammer doing an excellent job of silencing the conversation. It was not nearly as effective at blocking out her warmth and soft curves beckoning him, as he worked inches away from her lithe body. She, meanwhile, was so absorbed in the pages of her book that she seemed oblivious to both him and the noise.

He returned to the truck for the level and longer nails and, most importantly, to give himself space. When he came back, Veronica was still pushing against the post that no longer needed her support, while reading her instruction manual. His body hummed with awareness as he worked around her.

Finally, she closed the book and looked at him. "I should do the work while you tell me what I need to do for each step," she said. "Like most people, I learn faster and more completely by doing than by watching and listening."

He doubted her plans for after she left his company required any skills he could teach her. Then again, if he gave her the chance to touch the gate and get a splinter, maybe she'd decide her thirty-day trial wasn't worth it. He could get his focus back on completing jobs and bringing in new business. He had employees and bills to pay.

He handed over the hammer and the level, momentarily sidetracked as a breeze blew the scent of her exotic perfume — orchids, maybe, or mangos or…bleach? — to his nostrils. "Pound in the L brackets. Make sure they're straight."

Veronica accepted only the level, leaving him to hold the hammer. She took an inordinate amount of time making sure the brackets were lined up and the bubble in the level was perfectly positioned inside the lines. He gave her points for precision, even though patiently watching someone do the work he could do faster and better made him crazy.

Finally, she returned the level and took the hammer. She swung at the nail and…

She smashed her thumb against the post.

"Oh!" She gasped and her eyes filled with tears as the nail and bracket clattered to the ground. Instead of falling with them or turning to him, she bent and picked up the pieces. She took the level back out of his hand and started to repeat the process of positioning the bracket again.

Matt stared at her, trying to understand what had happened. She'd smashed her thumb, and now she was going to continue working without complaining? The pain had to be excruciating. Didn't this woman have a nasty side? Kimberly certainly had unleashed hers the first—and only— time she'd allowed herself close enough to physical labor to get a tiny scratch. At the very least, Veronica had the perfect opportunity to suck a little sympathy from him.

She silently traded the level for the hammer. This time she was more cautious with the tool, making contact with the nail using small, tentative strokes.

"You're not even denting the post," Matt pointed out.

She handed the hammer to him. "I think you should—"

She'd been so stoic earlier that he forced himself to swallow his smug "I told you so." He reached to take the hammer. She released it and crumpled to the ground.

"That's a delayed reaction if I ever saw one." And a little overdramatic as far as sympathy bids went. Matt looked down at her. She wasn't clutching her thumb. She was just…there.

He knelt beside her and placed his finger on the smooth, warm skin of her neck. Her pulse was steady. She'd just gone for an over-the-top attempt at sympathy.

Her eyes flickered open and settled on him. She started to sit up and immediately tucked her head in a fetal position. "I'm sorry." Her voice was muffled and weak. "I can hammer it. Give me a minute."

Okay, maybe this wasn't a sympathy bid at all. Maybe she really had fainted. "Do you need me to call an ambulance?"

"No, I'm fine. I'm going to finish hammering." She looked pale but was alert and insisting she was well enough to work.

He picked up the jug of water he'd brought with him, uncapped it, and levered her slowly into a sitting position, trying not to think about how intimately his hand was splayed up her back, his fingertips touching her spine. "Drink this."

She took a small sip and handed it to him. "Thanks."

He pushed it back to her. "Drink it like you mean it." He watched her throat work as she tipped her head to swallow, exposing flawless, pale skin. He managed to get half the contents in her before she returned the thermos, rewarding him with a little color in her cheeks.

He reached under her knees and around her back, lifting her up.

"What are you doing?" Her panicked voice was right against his ear.

He'd been platonically assisting an injured person. But her demand made him all too aware of their physical closeness. "Checking out your butt joints. What do you think?" he said with a laugh. "I'm carrying you to the truck, okay? I'm not making a move on you."

"Is there such a thing as thumb joints? That's where I could *really* use the attention." Veronica looped an arm around his shoulders and rested her head on his chest. He tucked his chin against the top of her head so he could lift the truck's passenger door handle.

His lungs filled with the strangely alluring scent of sodium hypochlorite and expensive perfume. He set her in the seat. If she'd stayed here to begin with, maybe he'd be able to concentrate on her thumb joint, instead of the other body parts he had no business touching but his fingers suddenly itched to explore. "Do you do this often?"

"Smash my thumb? I shut it in a door once. But this is my first time with a hammer." Her full pink lips were inches from his.

"Faint," he clarified, disentangling her arm from his shoulders and stepping back.

"Oh." Embarrassment gave her face more color. "Only once. I volunteered for Habitat for Humanity in the middle of July—crazy hot and humid. It was the first day, and they had us report to the site at some absurd hour, so I didn't have time for breakfast. I guess I kind of collapsed or something; I'm a little fuzzy on the details. All I know is they wouldn't let me touch the power tools after that. So I did paperwork, hit up vendors for donations, and coordinated charity events."

She had a history of passing out on the job. That definitely required documentation. And was exactly why he needed to return his focus to his employer responsibilities. "When was the last time you've eaten? I'm guessing you skipped breakfast?"

"Not on purpose. By the time I got my trailer clean enough that I could sleep in it, both the grocery store and that little diner on the corner were closed. I'd left my doughnuts outside, and some critter found them before I did. But I'm fine, Matt. Let me get back to work, please."

"Not on your life. Do you know how much my workman's comp insurance goes up when I have an on-the-job injury?" But as guilty as she was for not taking care of herself, he deserved just as much blame. He knew the state of her trailer made it impossible for her to cook anything, and he'd heard what the townspeople had done to her at the grocery store. She hadn't stepped inside Pauline's Diner, which, considering the gossip there, was probably a smart choice. And Barney likely would have sent her out of the convenience store with something completely inedible.

Clearly, she hadn't eaten since she arrived in Kortville yesterday. But he'd been too busy complaining about her being two minutes late for work and slowing him down on the job to notice. No wonder she'd passed out. Setting her up to fail was one thing—he would never purposefully endanger the health of anyone.

Matt was ashamed to realize he'd already done so. He slammed the passenger door, closed the tailgate, and settled into the driver's seat.

"Where are you taking me?"

Her suspicion was well founded. He'd already proven he couldn't be trusted to take care of her. "To get some food. And ice for your thumb."

She was cradling it in her other hand; he bet it was throbbing and giving her a splitting headache. Her inability to swing a hammer, however, had nothing to do with her state of nutrition. She had no business working construction if she couldn't drive a single nail into place.

"You left your tools behind," she noted as he backed out of the driveway. "We didn't finish hanging the gate, and I really wanted to meet the owner of that house."

"I'll come back and finish up. The job's almost done."

"So I'm your top priority." She leaned her forehead against the window. "That's so sweet."

His chest tightened, but he kept his voice impassive. "You have a warped idea of top priority if you think someone who makes you beat yourself up with tools and then pass out is sweet."

She lifted her head enough to smile weakly at him. "Matt Shaw, you are without a doubt the sweetest boss I've ever had."

His fingers twitched. He clenched the steering wheel, but it was a poor substitute for the skin he longed to touch. "You're only saying that because I haven't fired you yet."

Chapter Three

Her head was pounding nearly as hard as her thumb. Veronica kept her eyes closed, wishing she could shrivel and fade away. So she needed to remember to eat in the morning. So she wasn't cut out for construction. She had her wits. She had an MBA, for goodness sake! She could make it in the world.

The truck stopped moving, and Veronica looked out the windshield. They were stopped in front of another house, this one nearly as small as her trailer but much better maintained, the grass perhaps a day or two overdue for a mowing. "What are we doing here?"

"Getting breakfast. Can you walk?"

"Yes, I'm fine." Her cheeks heated. Matt had cradled her in his arms as he'd carried her to the vehicle. If he'd given her a minute, she could have walked. But instead, he'd proven his theory of how helpless she was and given her a taste of how *good* it felt to be helpless in his big, strong arms.

She was pathetic, finally claiming her pride and independence only to toss it aside less than twenty-four hours later, the second she stumbled upon a cute guy. She got out of the pickup and walked under her own power, but Matt hovered inches from her, ready to catch her if she so much as stumbled while she made her way to the front door. "Whose house is this?"

"Mine." He unlocked the door and held it open for her.

She made no move to step over the threshold. She wasn't going to depend on him to take care of her. She could take care of herself. "Take me to my trailer, please. I'll find something to eat."

"I saw what your refrigerator was stocked with. How do you feel about omelets?"

"Too much work. How about a piece of toast?" Okay, she'd eat here. He was right about the lack of anything edible in her trailer. A little food, and she'd be able to think more clearly. She had to convince him she had something to offer as an employee so he wouldn't want to fire her.

She stepped inside. Matt closed the door behind her and headed through the small entry into the living room. She followed him through the open floor plan to the kitchen. She was wrong. The house looked small from the outside, but it was at least twice the size of her trailer.

He pulled out a chair at the table and gestured for her to sit. Then he set an ice pack, a towel, and a glass of orange juice in front of her. "How's the thumb? Are you going to lose the fingernail?"

"Lose my nail?" She sank into the offered chair, feeling woozy again. Her thumb was red and puffy, but the ice felt heavenly.

"Stick around, and it'll happen," Matt said. "This is construction, not a tea party."

Matt opened the refrigerator and began pulling out eggs, sausage, ham, mushrooms, peppers, onions, broccoli, and cheese. The appliance appeared well stocked for a guy who ate coffee and doughnuts on the run. And Matt looked as comfortable chopping vegetables and tossing ingredients in the pan as he did swinging a hammer.

His brown hair curled around the neckline of his white tee, which stretched across his broad shoulders every time he reached along the counter. One back pocket of his jeans showed off a square white outline of his wallet. He flipped the omelet onto a plate and set two slices of buttered toast along the side.

Then he turned away from the stove to face her, his brown eyes intense but gentle. His sensuous, full mouth curved slightly, outlined by his square jaw. He slid the plate across the table to her. "Eat. When you're done, you can rest on the couch while I go back to the farmhouse."

Veronica blinked. She'd assumed he'd stay while she ate, that maybe he'd share part of her meal; there was no way she could eat all of it. In any event, she had to return to the job site with him. "You're going to leave me here?"

"I have things to do."

She needed to work, too, so she could make enough money to afford her next meal and not pass out again. "Give me fifteen minutes, and I'll come with you."

She lifted a forkful of egg up to her mouth, and her taste buds screamed in delight at the delicious flavors. "Oh my gosh; this is so good. You have to try a bite."

His gaze softened. "I have tried it. Trust me, it wasn't that good the first time I made it…or even the tenth." He dropped into the chair next to her. "Why don't you take the rest of the day off to build your strength up, then you can hit the ground running tomorrow?"

"I hope that was an expression, and you don't actually have a marathon planned." She made a face, still attempting to eat quickly instead of savoring each bite, so she could help him fix the gate.

He rose to his feet. "No marathon, I promise. But you have to take care of yourself, because no one is going to do it for you."

She looked from her omelet to him, her insides warming. "I think you just did."

"Did you come here looking for a man to take care of you? Because if that's the case, you might as well tell Ron you want to end this job experiment."

Warmth deserted her. Pampering and coddling were the last things she wanted, especially from her boss. "I'm ready to go back to work right now."

Matt frowned at her half-eaten meal. "Not until you've finished every bite of that and rested. I'll come back and check on you at noon." With that, he marched out of the house.

She ran to the door in time to see the pickup peel out of the driveway. He'd stranded her, but he must trust her, too. He wouldn't have left her alone in his house otherwise, right? The thought made her smile as she looked around. Matt's house had a definite masculine brown and cream color theme going. But it wasn't completely sterile. The dishtowel hanging over the handle of the stove had a gaudy orange rooster on it. A flash of pink peeked out from under the edge of the worn couch.

Her heart stopped and then thundered. How would she explain to his girlfriend what she was doing in his house if the woman returned before he did or before Veronica left? Knowing she was snooping, she walked to the couch and pulled on the scrap of pink. A Barbie throw pillow and *Charlotte's Web* appeared. Not from a girlfriend. A daughter, maybe? Of course, that meant a wife was likely in the picture, too.

She pushed the offending book and pillow back under the couch and returned to the table to finish her brunch.

Then she took her dishes to the sink and her ice pack to the freezer. She paused with her hand on the refrigerator door. A child's drawing of a man and a young girl holding hands was attached with magnets. The child's writing labeled the man UNCLE MATT and the girl JENNY. In the top corner next to the sun were two tiny people with wings and the heart-stopping words, MOMMY AND DADDY IN HEAVEN.

Veronica's eyes filled with tears, and she felt an overwhelming urge to hold and comfort this girl, who'd endured an unspeakable tragedy in her young life. But of course, she didn't need Veronica's comfort; she already had Matt. Veronica had no doubt he was doing everything in his power to fill the gap and be both parents for his young niece.

Veronica set down her dishes and dabbed her eyes. Then she washed the plate and cup and wiped the counter. Matt probably assumed she would leave her mess for him to clean up. He seemed so sure she wanted to be pampered that it felt important to prove she could hold her own without an entourage to care for her. She'd already confirmed his belief that she needed someone to look after her on the job.

After that, the couch was too inviting to resist. She lay down, only for a minute until her headache was gone.

The next thing she knew the shadows were coming from the other direction, and a blanket covered her body. Her headache was gone. The pain in her thumb had subsided to a dull, forgettable ache.

She had no idea how long she'd slept. But clearly, it had been substantially longer than a minute. She started to fold the blanket and paused. Matt must have come to check on her, as he'd promised, and covered her while she was sleeping. She tried to envision the look on his square, tan, handsome face as he'd settled the blanket over her. Tenderness, perhaps? Maybe he was starting to care about her.

Or was he simply disgusted that she was sleeping all day when she should have been working? She sighed at the more likely scenario and set the blanket on the end of the couch. It was time to figure out how to get home—her trailer home.

She had no idea where Matt's house was in relation to the rest of town—she'd kept her eyes closed on the ride over. At the time, it had seemed like the only way to keep her headache at bay.

All right. She might not have her GPS, and she didn't trust the townspeople to give her directions to anywhere but the interstate, but the town was small and she was wearing comfortable shoes. She'd find her way—to the house with the broken gate, to the convenience store, or to the Kortville Construction office. Wherever she arrived first, that's where she'd put in her time. Then she'd go home.

After twenty minutes of walking, her toes pinched and her boots felt like torture chambers instead of practical, comfortable footwear, but she knew where she was. She could see the convenience store sign. Perfect. She'd cover the doughnuts and spend the rest of the day hanging drywall and spreading joint compound.

The plan lost a little of its perfection when she got closer and saw that Matt's truck wasn't in front of the store. Her anticipation over the job disappeared without him to share it. She couldn't stop thinking about him walking in and covering her with that blanket, instead of demanding she wake up and get back to work—which he would have been well within his rights to do. If her father or Trevor had been half as thoughtful, she might never have left home.

She limped through the parking lot, favoring her brand-new blisters. The convenience store door was propped open with the beer boxes again. She tried to convince herself this was the best-case scenario: she'd finish the job. When Matt saw what she'd accomplished, he'd realize she was an asset to his team, not someone he needed to babysit.

"Look who's here." Barney hustled around the counter to her side. "Just the person I wanted to see."

"I am?" She smiled, pleased that she was making headway with the townspeople.

"Absolutely. My freezer was accidentally unplugged all night, and I have this box of ice cream bars that I need to give away." Barney lifted a box. The corners were discolored, damp, and squishy.

She couldn't allow for a repeat of yesterday. "Thanks, Barney, but I actually came here to polish off the remodeling project for Matt."

"I thought you were spending the day lounging on his couch."

Matt had told everyone she was a slacker. Nice.

"Anyway, I hired *him*, not you. Have some ice cream." He held out the box, which dripped a steady stream of white cream onto the gray concrete between them.

"You hired Kortville Construction," she corrected, doing her best to pretend she didn't see his *gift*. "I am an employee of the company."

"You've got to take this ice cream and get it out of here right now. It's making a big mess on my floor." He shoved the cold, gooey box against her chest and nudged her toward the door.

Ick. She much preferred the dusty doughnuts. "Barney, I'm going to give this box back to you if you don't explain to me why you won't consider one single thing I ask for when I come inside your store."

"I don't know what you're talking about." His face was a picture of pudgy innocence.

She held out the box, and the ice cream stopped soaking

her shirt and starting pooling on the floor.

"Okay, okay." He pushed the box back against her again. "You're ruining everything. You think I'm remodeling because I've got money to throw around? No, I'm spiffing this place up because it's going to be *the* place to hang out. People will grab Gatorade, doughnuts, ice cream, pizza—everything they need for the big game."

"The big game?"

He pointed across the street. "Ron promised to clear out the trailers and donate the old trailer park for a community baseball field. People were going to start playing ball this summer. By next spring he was going to donate the funds for lights, so they could play night games. Kids' leagues, adult leagues, teams from neighboring towns. They were all going to come here, and they were going to get gas and snacks at my store."

She tried to envision it, but her sticky, wet shirt stole her concentration. "And I'm living on third base?"

He almost smiled. "Over home plate, actually."

"Well, that's a problem," she agreed, giving him her brightest smile. "But this is only temporary, Barney. I don't want to live in that trailer forever. Hopefully, long before next spring, I'll have solved my income problem and I'll have a nice little house far enough away that I won't have stray foul balls coming through my windows."

He didn't look appeased. "If you're here at all, working for Ron's distribution warehouse, that means he didn't sell it, so he won't have the cash lying around to pay for the lights like he'd promised—not to mention the new library building, the community closet, or the food pantry."

"Ron promised all that?" Despite offering her a job, he hadn't struck her as the most generous of men.

"He's willing to give money to every cause. He just needs

to sell his business before he has the cash to fund everything."

And if she took over, his money would be tied up and unavailable for distribution. Ugh. No wonder everyone hated her. She couldn't just give up the job Ron had promised her to make them happy—she needed it to build her own foundation. She deserved that as much as they deserved a new baseball field or library building. But now guilt warred with her ambitions. She'd never imagined that she'd be taking away things that others needed to meet her own goals.

Veronica took off her sticky shirt and cleaned up the mess from Barney's ice cream before donning a clean knit top. She couldn't make any of the same missteps tomorrow that she'd made today. That meant she needed to find out from Matt if the start time varied by day or if it was always at seven a.m. and where she should meet him. She rummaged through her purse for her phone and dialed.

"Kortville Construction. This is Matt."

"Hi, Matt, this is Veronica."

"Hey." He sounded a lot less welcoming.

She forced herself to maintain the same level of cheerfulness. She wouldn't let his lack of enthusiasm rub off on her. "Is your house intact? No one ran off with the good silver while she had free run of the place?"

"My niece can't find her Barbie pillow. Otherwise, we're fine."

"Under the couch," Veronica answered automatically.

He was quiet, probably mentally picturing her snooping under each piece of furniture.

She hurried to change the subject and keep her tone lighthearted. "I called to check on the agenda for tomorrow.

What macho job do you have planned for me?"

"We're stripping a roof."

"Excuse me?" She'd tolerated blatant discrimination from the townspeople, her parents' barbaric beliefs about marriage and working women, and Barney's twisted ideas of edible gifts, but Matt had crossed the line. She absolutely was not going to stand for it. "If you want to see me naked so badly that you think you can make up a job where I have to strip on anyone's roof—"

His booming laughter interrupted her tirade. "You obviously didn't get to that chapter in your book yet. Stripping a roof is ripping off the old shingles, not your clothes."

"Oh." Of *course* it was an incomprehensible industry term. She'd made herself sound like a complete idiot and a shrew to boot. "I-I forgot my book when I left the job this morning. I'll get it, so I can study up tonight."

"I have it in my truck," Matt said, his laughter subsiding but his voice still full of amusement.

"Oh," she said again. She wasn't sure what she thought about him picking up after her. It wasn't quite as sexy as tucking a blanket around her shoulders as she slept, but no matter how much he protested, taking care of other people was clearly second nature to him.

"Do you mind if I drive over to your house and get it?" she asked. She definitely wasn't going to walk, not with the way her feet were killing her from making the trip earlier.

"I'm pulling into the diner now. I'll swing by your trailer and drop it off after I'm done eating."

Pauline's Diner. It was dinnertime. She shouldn't have been hungry for a week after that magnificent omelet, but her stomach growled anyway. "I need to eat, too. I'll meet you at the diner."

"Veronica?" Matt stopped her before she hung up. There

was a hint of mirth in his voice.

"Yeah?"

"If I wanted to see you naked, I wouldn't need to get you on a roof. All I'd have to do is look through your bedroom window."

. . .

"Come on, Uncle Matt. What's taking so long?" Jenny tugged on his hand.

Matt pocketed his phone and allowed her to drag him out of his truck toward the diner entrance. He wished he could take back that last comment he'd made to Veronica. Whether she needed curtains on her windows or not, he shouldn't have flirted with her. He was her boss, and his impressionable niece was within earshot.

"Hey, my favorite couple." Pauline greeted them with a wide smile as they stepped inside the restaurant. "Take a seat, and I'll be right with you. You're in luck. I'm trying out a bunch of new espresso recipes today."

Jenny led him to a table in the middle of the restaurant. He raised a hand in greeting to the chairwoman of the library board and her husband in a booth near the door and a family from Jenny's school at the table next to them. All of them gave him a subtle headshake on the espressos.

Jenny picked the seat facing the door. Matt settled in across from her as Pauline bustled back. "I have cinnamon-mocha-apple, caramel pistachio, cherry-vanilla-squash, and hazelnut parfait espressos," she said.

"We'll just have the usual," Matt told her.

"Are you sure?" Pauline's enthusiasm deflated. "These espressos are the best yet."

"Grilled cheese is the best," Jenny declared.

The usual meant milk to drink, along with grilled cheese for Jenny and the cook's nightly special for Matt. Liver and onions was the only meal that Matt couldn't stomach, and only on those nights did he reluctantly venture into trying Pauline's bizarre concoctions.

Pauline set out two glasses and uncapped the jug of milk. The front door jingled, and she poured the milk right over the rim of his glass.

"You're overflowing," he said, since she didn't appear to notice. The white liquid headed straight for his lap.

She set down the jug and handed him a stack of napkins, all with her gaze locked on the front door. "Oh my gosh. The city girl has come to my diner!" She rushed across the room to pump Veronica's hand. "You are going to *love* my espressos, honey."

"Uh, thanks. You can call me Veronica." She shot Matt a questioning glance, as Pauline led her to a table directly in front of the door.

"I'm going to let you try one of each flavor." Pauline rattled them off again. "And you have to give me your honest-to-goodness opinion if they're better than what you drink in those fancy coffee shops, okay?"

"Um, sure. May I order some food, too?" Veronica's eyes lit up with amusement as she smiled at Pauline.

"We'll get to that. The good stuff comes first." She bustled away.

Veronica's gaze flicked around the room, where no one would meet her eye. When her gaze came to him, Matt nearly laughed out loud. "Welcome to the diner."

Her eyes widened. "Are these espressos like Barney's 'gifts' from the convenience store?" she whispered.

"Nope. Pauline doesn't play favorites. She'll try out her concoctions on anyone who's not quick enough to order the nightly special."

Pauline came back before Veronica could reply and set four mugs and saucers in a row in front of her, along with a pen and an inch-thick stapled booklet.

Jenny's eyes widened. "Uncle Matt, she's not really going to taste test, is she? Someone has to warn her."

"I think it's too late," Matt murmured back as Pauline opened to the first page in the booklet.

"See this checklist? I want you to rate each of these drinks on a scale of one to ten based on the criteria on the paper. I doubt it would happen, but just in case, if you rate anything less than a ten, please write an explanation below. I have extra blank pages in the back if you need more space." Pauline smiled widely at her.

"Okay," Veronica said uncertainly.

"I need to check on the rest of my customers. I'll be right back." Pauline hurried away, a spring in her step.

Veronica raised an eyebrow at Matt.

He shrugged, but his stomach felt queasy. "If you want, whisper to her to mark everything perfect tens," he said to Jenny.

"I'll spill a couple on the floor, too, so she doesn't have to drink them all," Jenny said, jumping to her feet.

That wasn't such a great idea, but Jenny had run off before he could say so.

She reached the table at the same time that Pauline did. "You only gave the cherry-vanilla-squash an 'eight' for smoothness? Why didn't it deserve a ten?" Pauline demanded. "I used real cherries, none of that cheesy syrup the other places use."

"Oh, I could tell that immediately," Veronica said, tipping a cherry pit off her spoon onto the saucer. "I really like your decision to go with natural flavors. You're right—it's so much classier than the syrup, but it's also a bit more challenging to make the drink smooth. I can tell you're a woman who's up to a good challenge."

Matt stared openly as she smiled at Pauline and winked at Jenny, who was now standing next to her. Jenny hadn't had a chance to warn her, but Veronica had turned the less-than-perfect score into a kudos for Pauline, all while smiling as if this behavior was exactly the kind of service she'd expected when she entered the restaurant.

"Would you like to order a grilled cheese?" Jenny suggested.

"I'd love to. Pauline, you have a fabulous helper here."

Oh boy. Now Veronica wasn't just pushing Pauline's buttons. She was going after his. Anyone who could see what a great kid he was raising earned his instant goodwill.

Pauline grunted. "Do you think putting the cherries in a blender instead of throwing them in whole would help?"

"I'm not really a helper. I just come here a lot with my uncle Matt. My name's Jenny," she said.

"I've met your uncle Matt," Veronica said to her. She smiled over his niece's head at him. "He makes a mean omelet."

Matt's insides became uncomfortably warm, and he shifted in his chair.

But Veronica had already looked away from him, back to Pauline. "I think the blender will improve the smoothness a lot. I'm sure you've already thought of this, but just remember to take out the pits before you blend. You wouldn't want to sacrifice your perfect ten on taste just to get the desired smoothness."

Matt nearly laughed out loud, but Veronica managed to deliver her suggestion with a straight face.

"Would you like to sit at our table, so you're not all

alone?" Jenny asked hopefully.

Matt's attraction morphed into unease. He'd always made sure his niece had women in her life—teachers, babysitters, her friends' mothers—so she wouldn't feel the sting of growing up without a mother or need to fill the void with an inappropriate role model. Yet, it had taken mere seconds for her eyes to fill with hero worship and adoration.

"She's not alone." Pauline sat down across from Veronica. "Now tell me, have you ever had a hazelnut parfait espresso before?"

"I have not. Perhaps...I might not be qualified to judge this one," Veronica said, shooting Matt a hopeful glance.

"Nonsense. I'll talk you through it," Pauline said.

"*Charlotte's Web* is my favorite book," Jenny declared, a look of desperation on her face.

"Really? What's your favorite part? Mine is when Fern saves the baby pig and feeds him with a bottle," Veronica said.

"No way. That's mine, too!" She swung her arm in exaggerated excitement and nearly knocked over a few of the espresso mugs.

Matt needed to call Jenny back to his table. She was getting out of hand, and Veronica seemed to be handling Pauline better on her own than anyone else he'd ever witnessed.

Pauline caught Jenny's hand and saved the drinks. "Why don't you run to the kitchen and ask Tom to make a grilled cheese. Tell him to bring your food to your table when it's ready, too."

Jenny frowned for a moment but then scurried off.

The rest of the patrons openly gaped as Veronica patiently smiled and nodded her way through Pauline's dissertation. She must have caught on quickly, Matt mused, because she rated everything about the hazelnut parfait a dazzling ten.

Jenny came back through the dining room carrying a

plate with grilled cheese and plopped it between the espresso mugs and Veronica. The cups tipped, and Pauline lunged to protect her precious drinks, but she overcorrected, dumping everything on the sandwich plate.

Jenny stared in horror. "Not the grilled cheese! You were supposed to eat that. I'm sorry," she whispered.

Veronica jumped up as the liquid spilled over the edge of the table, leaving wet splotches on her jeans. "Jenny, is that offer still open to sit at your table?" she asked a bit desperately. "I think I'd like to take you up on it if your uncle doesn't mind."

"Let me get you more to drink," Pauline said, standing up as well.

"Oh, you don't need to go to the trouble. Just a glass of water would be wonderful," Veronica said.

"You don't like my espressos?" Pauline pouted.

"I do! In fact, I gave them all tens."

"But you didn't even try them all," Pauline said.

"I'm sure they would have been wonderful. If you have more you'd like me to try, I will. But if you don't, I understand."

That was definitely the wrong thing to say. Matt knew it even before Pauline sprang into action.

"Stay there. I'll be right back." Pauline bustled behind the counter.

"I was trying to save you from the drinks. I didn't mean to ruin your sandwich," Jenny said.

Veronica turned to her and squeezed her hand. "Thank you for trying to save me, for the fabulous table service, and for the grilled cheese, which I'm certain would have been delicious. You are the most welcoming, sweetest person I have met in this entire town. Your uncle must be very proud of you."

"Follow me," Pauline called. "I'm going to set you up in a

booth in the back, so no one will disturb us."

Veronica turned her gaze to Matt. He was absurdly proud—not just of Jenny but of Veronica's ability to remain poised and regal.

"If you like, you can bring my home-improvement book to me when you're finished with your meal. I'm going to hazard a guess that I'll be here much longer than you. If you'd prefer not to interfere in the taste test, you can drop it off at my trailer. I left it unlocked."

Of course she'd left it unlocked. She had no lock. Or door.

Veronica followed Pauline to the back of the restaurant before he could reply. Jenny stared after her, her eyes round and adoring.

"I can't believe how rude city customers are," the chairwoman of the library board muttered. "Only an 'eight,' just because of a tiny cherry pit. What was she thinking?"

Jenny leaned toward Matt and clutched his hand. "Can I have a pink bandana for my hair like she had in hers? Please?"

Matt groaned. "I'll look around and see if we have one. But now you need to sit down and eat your grilled cheese."

"Can we invite her over for dinner at our house? I have important questions to ask her."

"Really? What do you need to know that you can't learn from me?"

"About makeup and high heels," Jenny said, taking a bite of her sandwich.

Just like that, Matt's appetite was gone. Jenny's mother hadn't worn a stitch of makeup or owned a pair of high heels. Steve and Leah had entrusted Matt to instill in Jenny their hardworking, wholesome values—values that didn't include an entitled mentality and frivolous wants. If Pauline's espressos didn't drive Veronica out of town, he was going to have to push much harder to show her that the only thing she was going to get handed to her here was hard work, dusty doughnuts, and coffee with hidden cherry pits.

Chapter Four

The next morning, Veronica was wide awake early, thanks to Pauline's never-ending supply of espressos. She ate a granola bar and a protein shake, the best she could do in her dysfunctional kitchen. She wouldn't pass out for any reason today. Matt was going to see that she could hold her own in his world.

Judging from yesterday, T-shirts were the construction ensemble of choice, so she dressed in a pink Ralph Lauren design with jeans, along with her denim blazer, since the air blowing in her open window was chilly. The thumb she'd smashed yesterday was bruised but didn't bother her as long as she was careful with it.

She covered her feet with Band-Aids and put on her black boots. Sneakers would have been more comfortable, but she'd already figured out that boots were expected in this industry. Matt needed to see her as a professional, so instead of waiting for him to pick her up at her trailer, she drove to the Kortville Construction office to meet him.

His truck was already parked in front of the small building across the street from the diner. She strolled inside and almost turned and dashed out again. Papers were strewn everywhere. A large desk in the middle of the room had teetering stacks nearly two feet high that completely obscured a computer monitor. If a keyboard was underneath the piles, she saw no sign of it.

"What are you doing here?" Matt stepped into the hallway from farther back in the dusty, dingy building.

"Thinking of hiring a cleaning service," she teased. "I assume you have a method to all this and you don't have a secretary smothered under these stacks?"

"I haven't checked, but I assume not, since we haven't had a missing persons case in Kortville for a while." He stepped closer. "What have you eaten today?"

"I ate." She glanced over the piles on the desk. One section was a stack of unopened bank statements. Her fingers twitched to open the envelopes and reconcile the number on the statement to the actual balance in his account.

"I don't want a repeat of yesterday. I think you should stay home and rest."

And not make it to day two, let alone day thirty? Not a chance. "Yesterday I needed carbs and protein, which you provided in stunning fashion. Do you know you're the first man to cook for me?"

Awareness flared in Matt's eyes but when he spoke, his tone was clipped. "Carbs and protein were *all* I offered."

He'd actually offered her a lot more: on the floor of the trailer, laughter so strong it made her forget all her worries. The companionship of his adorable niece when she was overwhelmed with Pauline's intensity. And the sweetness to go above the call of duty and open his home and his kitchen to her.

"It wasn't a date, and I won't cook for you again," he finished emphatically.

"Gotcha, boss." If he wanted to go the all-business route, she could suck up and accommodate. "I am one hundred percent prepared for this roofing job. I did a lot of reading last night. You're going to be so impressed."

He raised his eyebrows.

Okay, she'd probably gone a little over the top. "After today, though, you might want to think about putting me to work in the office." Her blisters would weep with thanks. "I'm good at analyzing business plans and determining their profitability potential. I think I could probably even find your computer under that mess and show you how to turn it on."

"What good would that do if I'm not going to use it for anything? I already have a fine handle on which jobs are the most profitable."

"Most business owners think so," she agreed, not the least bit intimidated by his curt tone. She'd seen how tenderly he dealt with his niece following the espresso-soaked grilled cheese incident in the diner. "It's always interesting to see where the numbers meet your expectations and which ones surprise you."

He was getting annoyed; she could see it in the tightness of his mouth. All of a sudden, she wanted to kiss it until it relaxed again.

"Anyway," she rushed on before he could speak or she could act on her impulses, "you can think about it while we strip that roof."

The awareness sprang to life in his eyes again. Her heart jumped when she realized that maybe he wasn't thinking about ripping off shingles any more than she was.

• • •

Matt parked his truck on the street in front of the single-story home with attached garage. The Dumpster he'd ordered was sitting in the driveway, and the new shingles hadn't arrived yet but were on their way. He glanced across the cab, wondering for the fifteenth time how Veronica had managed to produce something edible from her toxic kitchen. He refused to ask. It wasn't any of his business.

However, in case she hadn't eaten and was too proud to admit it, he said, "There's beef jerky in the glove compartment and a thermos of water by your feet. Sit down and help yourself if you start to feel light-headed."

She smiled as if he'd offered her a diamond necklace. "Thank you."

Man, she had a great smile. He was far from immune to its effect.

He jumped out of the truck and slammed the door to resist leaning toward her and doing something monumentally stupid like tasting that delectable smile. He stood at the side of the truck, taking several deep breaths before rounding the back bumper.

By the time he had his hormones under control, Veronica had beaten him there and was pulling down the tailgate. She wrestled the long metal extension ladder from the truck bed. It seesawed as she struggled to keep both ends off the ground at once.

Matt took an instinctive step to help her. But he wasn't her friend. He was her employer, and a reluctant one at best. He shoved his hands in his pockets and stepped back. The action kept him out of range of her shaky grip and from giving her a hand, but it didn't stop him from feeling guilty about making her do more than she could handle.

She staggered toward the house, the back end of the ladder banging against the side of the truck. "Oh, sorry. I didn't hit your truck, did I?" Veronica turned to look and nearly knocked him in the head with the long, unwieldy metal apparatus.

Matt ducked and inspected the damage. She'd given him a small ding near the gas door but had missed breaking his taillight…and his skull. "No damage. Just watch where you're going with that thing."

"I'm headed up on the roof with it, aren't I?"

He hauled the pitchforks out and then glanced in her direction. Veronica had leaned the ladder against the gutter over the front door. She put her foot on the first step without verifying the equipment's sturdiness, and it wiggled precariously. She ignored the warning and lifted her other foot.

"Stop!" Matt dropped the pitchforks and rushed toward the house. The ladder swayed.

He wasn't going to get to her in time. She was going to crash to the ground—for the second straight day. But Veronica continued to teeter for another moment, allowing him to reach her. He placed his hands on her legs, ignoring her soft sound of surprise, and snatched her off the ladder as it tipped sideways.

Matt clutched her, turning her body away from the falling metal in case it shattered the front windows. The ladder timbered harmlessly into the bushes instead. He could feel Veronica's heart thundering against his chest through both their shirts. Silky strands of her sweet-smelling hair curled around his face.

He was falling, and he wasn't going to land as gently as the ladder.

He pulled her back to arm's length. "What were you thinking?"

"You need a new ladder." Her voice was shaky, making him want to take her in his arms all over again. "They're not supposed to fall like that."

Matt fought the urge to tuck her body against his and reassure her while he soaked in her warmth and softness. He made himself think about the expense and hassle of replacing the extension ladder. After a moment of concentration, the urge to hold her shifted into a need to shake some sense into her. Better. He could harness that energy.

"The ladder works the way it was intended." At least it had before it toppled to the ground. "You need to learn how to set it up correctly. I'll bring you the owner's manual and you can read up on it tonight. In the meantime, make sure any ladder is steady before you ever step foot on it."

• • •

After the ladder incident, Matt took over setting it up and testing its sturdiness. Veronica stood to the side and fiddled with her phone while she waited for him. Personally, she didn't see a need to continue. The house already had a roof, and it looked perfectly fine to her. She'd probably only highlight her ignorance if she mentioned it, though, so she concentrated on her phone instead.

She'd missed a call from Trevor's personal assistant. She considered immediately deleting it, but what if her parents were sick or injured and Paige was frantically trying to notify her? She took another step back and listened to the message.

"Veronica, this is Paige. Trevor asked me to check in with you. He's not sure what problem you're having with the engagement, but he thought you and I could talk and work things out. He has a full schedule of meetings today, but feel free to call me anytime and we can chat. The merger is very important to him."

How could anyone not understand their problem after

listening to a message like that? She didn't want to marry Trevor *or* his overworked office staff. She hit the delete key hard, wishing she'd gone with her instincts and done so before she'd listened. Then she turned off the phone and set it inside the truck.

"The ladder's secure now. Climb up," Matt said.

This was her alternative—a job she was unqualified for in fifty different ways with a boss who made her feel fifty million times more than she'd ever felt for her father's designated heir apparent.

She took a deep breath and started gingerly up the first step. It didn't wiggle. Matt's hand on the metal rail gave her additional confidence to climb until she was eye level with the shingles. Some were a little curled, but she couldn't find any gaping holes.

"Move on so I can come up, too," he called.

The book hadn't mentioned any tips about coping with heights and steep slopes, but she couldn't wimp out before she'd started. She moved her hands forward and put a knee on the shingles. Standing on the dangerously sloped surface was out of the question, but she could probably crawl high enough to get out of Matt's way.

"Don't go too far. I need to hand the equipment up to you."

She was no expert, but that likely involved looking down. "What are the chances I'll fall over the edge?"

"Slim, as long as you don't dangle by your feet from the gutters. Grab the pitchfork when it comes up." Although he sounded like he was rolling his eyes at her, he lifted the pronged metal tool high enough that she didn't have to look down. Unfortunately, more tools followed—another pitchfork, two hammers, a bucket, and—

"What is that?" She stared as two handles and a big metal

tub rose in front of her.

"A wheelbarrow. Take it. Hurry."

She grabbed the handles, but it was heavy, and she was terrified she was going to plunge face-first onto the unforgiving concrete walkway below.

Matt climbed the ladder, pushing the bottom of the wheelbarrow with him onto the rooftop. Veronica scrambled up the steep slope with the handles, while Matt laid the wheelbarrow tub upside-down on the shingles, its single wheel pointed toward the sky. Her knees felt weak, so she sat next to it. Maybe if she'd been raised for this kind of work since birth it would be different, but going on a roof was, well, something people hired a roofing company to do.

"Just making sure I'm steady before I start working," she assured Matt. Right now she didn't have enough nerve to slide to the edge of the roof and climb down the ladder to leave the job. There were absolutely no railings or other protective devices to make for safe working conditions.

He grabbed a pitchfork and shoved it underneath the roof material inches from where she was sitting. He leaned his weight on the fork's handle, then reached down with a gloved hand and ripped the shingle off.

"It looks the same underneath," Veronica said. The picture in the book had prepared her for bare wood.

"Yep, another layer." Matt worked the pitchfork again.

"Ah, so we're down to the underwear in your stripping scenario."

"Well, really the top layer was the sweater. Now we're down to the actual clothes." After a couple pokes, he popped out a chunk. It flew across the roof, revealing a black surface. "*This* is the underwear," he proclaimed. He ripped away the black paper-like material that she'd forgotten the real name of, exposing naked wood underneath.

"No matter what you call it, you're still not going to convince me this job is sexy," Veronica said. She stood slowly, brushing the grit from the back of her pants.

"If anyone can find a way, it's you."

She raised a brow, her heart beating faster. "Is that a compliment?"

"Just a fact. Pry the shingles up with a pitchfork." He went straight back to all-business mode.

She stood, frozen. He thought she was sexy in her gritty pants, denim work blazer, and wearing an expression of near terror?

"Be careful not to damage the plywood underneath. Pile them in the wheelbarrow. When it's full, throw it over the side of the roof into the Dumpster." He held the pitchfork out to her, as if nothing out of the ordinary had occurred.

She tried to copy his impersonal demeanor. "What are you going to do while I work? Go back to the office and clean your desk?" The state of his office intrigued her even more than the revelation that he just might find her attractive. She'd never be as good as Matt at the manual labor, but she *could* get his office in order. She could create an amazing filing system in a month's time.

"Trust me, there's plenty of roof for both of us."

Resigned, she took the pitchfork. It was clumsy and other than feeding Paul Bunyan his dinner, it seemed like a useless tool, regardless of what her book said. She poked at a shingle. Nothing. "Wouldn't a shovel work better?" She was pretty sure the book had recommended using one at some point. She at least understood the concept of a shovel.

"You have to get under them." Matt walked behind her and encircled her, covering her hands on the pitchfork handle. His tan biceps bulged in her peripheral vision; his breath caressed her neck. Her knees melted into Jell-O for reasons that had nothing to do with a sloping roof.

"You have to put your whole body into it." His uneven breathing against her ear made her unsure if he was talking about the job.

"That suggestion's not exactly helpful," she pointed out, trying to get back the lightness they'd been sharing. She needed him to back up and give her space to concentrate on the roof and not his warmth against her back. If she wanted to prove to her grandfather that she should be trusted with a bigger responsibility, she had to maintain a professional working relationship with Matt.

She attacked the shingles with double the gusto. Before she left this roof, she'd get him to see she was serious about making their temporary work relationship benefit both of them.

And if she were lucky, she'd work so hard she'd forget all about her inconveniently growing attraction to her boss, too.

• • •

Veronica had made some progress, evidenced by a small bare patch of roof she'd unearthed and the equally small pile of shingles at her feet. Matt pretended he wasn't watching her as he tore off the old roofing on the opposite side of the peak. She pulled up a couple shingles from the first layer and went back to chipping at the bottom layer with the pitchfork.

She stopped once to strip off her jacket, and he wished he hadn't brought up the clothing analogy when he'd explained the layers on the roof. Now he was too aware of how many layers she had to go before she reached bare skin. The pink shirt she'd just exposed would likely be filthy beyond redemption by the time the job was complete.

She pulled back another shingle with her hands. It broke

free, sending her staggering backward. But she didn't whine about how far beneath her the physical labor was—she didn't even glance at him.

Matt hadn't figured out exactly who Veronica was, but she'd already proven she was made of stronger stuff than Kimberly, who had turned up her nose at any job where he could have used a second pair of hands, whether it was pitching a tent or changing the oil in his truck. Despite her superficial tendencies, he'd loved her.

Then three years ago, life had thrown him a curveball when Steve and Leah died. He swallowed the lump that still lodged in his throat when he remembered the exact moment he'd gotten the call about the accident. As his girlfriend, Kimberly had put her life on hold long enough to accompany him out of her city comfort zone.

But when it became obvious his move home needed to be permanent for Jenny's sake and to save Kortville Construction from ruin, she'd let him know in no uncertain terms she wasn't the woman for the job, not when she had so many more appealing options than being a stepaunt and wife of a construction worker. Matt didn't expect Veronica to last anywhere near to the end of the month, but she'd already far exceeded his expectations for what she would put up with.

Matt took his overflowing wheelbarrow to the Dumpster, dangling it by its handles over the peak of the roof. When he turned around, Veronica was watching him. She didn't appear to be gathering her voice to tell him off. More than likely, she was about to beg for a break. He'd give her a nice long one in the shade and make sure she drank plenty of water, too.

"I'm ready to load that thing now," she said.

No break? All right, then. Kudos to her.

He wheeled it to her and took her pitchfork, widening the area with a few well-placed strokes and giving her a lot more garbage to fill the wheelbarrow with. She loaded only half of it before she set off along the peak.

She wobbled and steered like her blood alcohol was twice the legal limit, but she made it to the edge. She lifted the handles and…

The wheelbarrow vanished over the edge of the house.

Veronica screamed and stumbled.

She's going to fall off the roof. "Let go of the wheelbarrow!" Matt shouted.

He dashed to her, arriving as the wheelbarrow landed with a terrific *thud*. He stared down. That *thud* could have been her body. Instead it was his heart, pounding so hard his chest physically hurt.

Veronica froze next to him, hunkered down on her hands and knees.

He pulled her back from the edge to the middle of the peak and folded his arms around her. Her body was shaking from the close call. His was, too. She'd almost fallen off the roof, and it was his fault.

"I'm sorry." Instead of returning his embrace, she clutched her arms across her chest, leaving dirty prints on her shirt.

"Take a break. I should have known better than to let you dump the load—it was too heavy." His stomach twisted with guilt.

"Weren't you trying to make me chicken out?"

He didn't answer. Yes, he'd wanted evidence that she couldn't follow through, so Ron could call this ridiculous deal off. Each minute on the job brought her closer to destroying everything his town was counting on for future generations.

He made sure she was able to stand on her own and then walked back to the edge of the roof to look down at the Dumpster. The wheelbarrow was dented, and the axel looked bent. But if he got it out before it was buried in debris, it wouldn't be a total loss.

He returned to Veronica, his need to comfort her swirling in his head. She could use more reassurance, and he wanted to be the one to give it to her. But he needed her to admit she couldn't do it. He'd changed the course of his life to stay in town and save Kortville Construction from ruin. Because his brother's financial mess had been so awful, he hadn't been able to save it without bringing in Ron's investment, and now he was stuck with another rich girl. She'd proven she had more staying power beyond Kimberly's superficial personality, but she still didn't care that her presence put the entire town's future in jeopardy.

"If you can't do this, you have to tell Ron that you quit," he said gently. "A lot of people can't. It's nothing to be ashamed of."

"I'm sorry about the wheelbarrow. If the company can't afford a replacement, I'll buy one myself." There was a quiet dignity in her voice that didn't match the bright sheen threatening to spill out of her eyes. She walked to her work area and began picking up the loose shingles.

His stomach still in knots and conflicted over whether to hold her or treat her harshly enough that she'd quit immediately, Matt went back to hacking at his half of the roof, while watching her in his peripheral vision. She was more stubborn than he would have guessed. She couldn't offer anything to his company, yet she continued to put every ounce of effort into the roof as if she had something to prove.

Down on the street, a door slammed. A moment later, Matt's part-time worker, a high school student named Toby, popped his head above the eaves as he climbed the ladder. "Hey, man, I came to join you."

"Hey, Toby." Matt forced himself to relax so his employee wouldn't pick up on his tension. "Don't you have school today?"

"They let us out early—some kind of teacher's work day."

Matt narrowed his eyes. "Are you sure? The elementary school is in session all day, and if your sister finds out you were skipping to work again, she will chew me up one side and down the other."

"I'll handle Becca. You have your hands full." Toby flicked his gaze at Veronica and waggled his eyebrows. "I thought you said she'd have quit by now."

Matt just rolled his eyes.

"I saw Dwayne and Zack—they should be here with the shingles in fifteen minutes. Good thing I'm here. You guys have a long way to go before you're ready to nail them down." He picked up the pitchfork and went to work widening Veronica's part of the roof.

"Matt expected I would have quit already?" Veronica set down the pile of shingles she'd been holding and stared at Toby.

He cleared his throat and looked panicked. "I meant I was surprised you and Matt weren't working on the same area. If one person pries them loose and the other tosses them into the wheelbarrow, it goes faster. Where is the wheelbarrow, by the way?"

"Don't ask." Veronica smoothed her dirty T-shirt and held her hand out to Toby. "I don't think we've had the pleasure of meeting. I'm Veronica Jamison, Ron Walker's granddaughter."

"I've heard of you," Toby said carefully without shaking her hand. "Where are your work gloves?"

Matt turned and looked at Veronica. She wasn't wearing gloves. A sixteen-year-old kid had noticed right away, while Matt had watched her beat up her hands all morning and never gave it a thought.

"I didn't know I needed any until I started playing with shingles." She smiled as if it were no big deal. "It's on my to-do list for my lunch break. Matt does give you lunch breaks, right?"

"I have an extra pair in my backpack." Toby laid down the pitchfork. "I'll be right back." He took a couple steps and stopped in front of Matt. "I know you don't like her and with good reason, but man, if it were me, I'd have quit long before you turned my hands into hamburger." Toby sidestepped him and headed for the ladder.

Matt marched across the roof and grabbed Veronica's hands, shaking off the broken shingle pieces she'd picked up. Her knuckles were seriously scraped up, but she'd never said a word. He flipped her hands palm up. They were filthy, of course, and blistered, with an oozing scratch on her left palm. Two blisters had already broken.

He looked up at her sweaty, dirt-streaked face and wished she would let him have it. Throw in his face that back in her real life, she'd never have given him the time of day. Say something about how she should get work credit while sitting in a lawn chair sipping lemonade. Anything so he could legitimately be angry with her and not feel like he was kicking a puppy. "Why didn't you say anything?"

She stuck her chin out with determination. "So you can laugh at me for skipping over a chapter in my book? No thanks."

"I am not laughing at any body part that looks like it's been put through a blender."

"I'm doing the work," she shot back. "Not as well or as fast as you—but I'm doing it, and I'll get it done."

"When was your last tetanus shot?"

She pulled her hands free. "I'm current, and I can take care of myself."

Not with the way he was working her over. Kimberly had packed up and gone home after Matt, overwhelmed with his new responsibilities, had made it clear he needed her to pitch in and meet him halfway. He'd counted on the same from Veronica. He'd underestimated this woman, and *that* scared him more than he wanted to admit. "I'm the boss, and I say you are done for the day."

Tears welled in her eyes. "My grandfather gave me the job. If—if you fire me, he'll hire me back."

Matt wasn't firing her. He was giving her a break, one that she deserved, and he was trying to apologize while still retaining an appropriate boss-employee distance instead of holding her in his arms. "I would never do a roofing project without gloves. I didn't offer you a pair or check if you brought your own. I failed in my on-the-job training. I'm going to take you home and help you clean those scrapes. The last thing I need is you getting an infection that goes on my conscience."

"Oh, you have a conscience? Learn something new every day." She brushed by him toward the ladder.

He hadn't killed her spunk. Matt smiled.

Despite trying not to, she'd made him like her anyway. Under different circumstances, he could imagine it growing into something more.

"Toby, thanks for the offer of gloves, but I'm going home," Veronica said from the top of the ladder. "If I can get down."

"Turn around and go backward, feet first. You're doing great." Toby talked her through each step. He praised her work on the roof and said all the nice things Matt should have said if he'd been smart enough to try to sweet-talk her into quitting. Or considerate enough to act like a real boss.

By the time her feet were on the ground, Veronica and Toby were joking about the piles of papers in the office and the wheelbarrow she'd dropped in the Dumpster. "Do you need a ride home?" he asked.

"To the office would be great. Matt can concentrate on fixing his wheelbarrow, which will hopefully put him in a better mood for the next batch of people he orders around."

"I'm driving her." Matt glared down the ladder at Toby. "You get Zack and Dwayne to help you finish clearing the roof."

"Sure, boss." Toby's look indicated he thought Matt's reasons for staying with Veronica didn't have much to do with a guilty conscience at all.

Only a real jerk would take advantage of a woman after she was bruised and battered from the work he'd forced on her. Of course, Matt had already proven himself a first-class jerk.

$$\cdots$$

Veronica held her throbbing hands in her lap and stared out the window. This shortened workday drive with Matt was becoming too familiar. She had to get away from him. She couldn't continue to put up the facade that all was fine when she could only sit and catalog her blistered hands, dirty face, and tattered clothes.

She was an embarrassment to the Jamison name. For that matter, the Walker name, too. Her grandfather couldn't be too proud of the walking disaster she'd become on her first two days on the job. Even the guys who mowed her parents' lawn wore gloves.

She'd known when she drove into town that she was going to work for a construction company. She should have bought gloves. In bulk. But she'd been so focused on what she was going to do with her life after the thirty days, she hadn't considered the details of how she would get through a month of manual labor.

Matt stopped the truck in front of her trailer. The loose end of the duct tape slapped in the breeze against the broken front window. By the time she worked up the energy to reach for the handle, he had rounded the hood and opened the door. He held out his hand to her.

"It's a little late to be chivalrous." And it was easier to pretend she was strong when he treated her like an employee and not a friend.

"It's a little late to pretend the work you're doing here is better than whatever life you had before."

"Touché." He was a tough-love friend—something she hadn't experienced before. And she appreciated it.

Veronica ignored his hand and limped for the front door. The funny thing was this *was* better. For the first time she felt like she was working toward something meaningful. She felt alive. Not that she enjoyed the torturous task of pulling shingles or the way her hands and feet hurt so badly that she wanted to cry. But it was certainly better than trying to earn her father's respect or maintain a relationship with Trevor through his assistant.

She reached for the screen door. "You don't have to wait for me. I'm going to stay away from the job site for the rest of the day."

Matt held the door open and stepped into the trailer behind her. "Wash your hands; I'll stay and help you medicate them. You're not going to be able to bandage them by yourself."

"I'm a disaster. I need to do more than just wash my hands. Since I don't have a tub to take a nice long bubble bath in, I'm going to shower. And you're not hanging out in my trailer while I do."

"Are you sure you don't need me to scrub your back?

Dirt gets into weird places on these jobs." He winked at her.

Veronica blinked at the fantasy that engulfed her, one that wasn't just sexual. They could work side by side and then come home and care for each other when the day was done. They could build a life together...

Asking out her boss was a social faux pas she knew better than to make. But allowing men to hold the power and to control her life was a mistake she'd made before. She could not fall for Matt if it meant giving up the dreams she was working so hard to make come true.

. . .

Matt held the screen door open as he backed out of the trailer, feeling like a first-class idiot to go along with his jerk status. She might as well throw the sexual harassment suit at him now. He certainly had it coming. "Sorry, that was inappropriate. I didn't mean to make you uncomfortable."

"You didn't. Thanks for the warning about the dirt."

He cleared his throat. Right. That's all he'd been getting at. "I'm going to run to the office for the first-aid kit. Open the screen door to let me know when you're dressed and ready for me to come back in."

Veronica's gaze stayed on him for a beat. "I don't think it's a good idea for you to come back—"

"I insist. Your wounds need to be attended to. The last thing I need is OSHA breathing down my neck."

"As long as it's work required," she said with a smile. Then she turned away and disappeared down the hall, the latch on the bathroom door echoing in her wake. She might be clueless about construction, but she proved she had heaps more common sense than he did.

He secured the flimsy screen in the door frame and then

turned around and surveyed the lawn. The door he'd broken two days ago was nowhere in sight. In fact, her yard was the only spot in the whole overgrown trailer park that didn't have a single dandelion in it. He couldn't imagine her taking on the task of weeding. Maybe the door had killed them all when it fell on them.

Where was that door, anyway? He'd promised to fix it on his next free evening. Of course, he'd also expected she'd be gone before he ever got a night to himself. He circled the trailer and found the door propped against the back wall next to a sizeable pile of limp green weeds and the remains of a sunflower pinwheel. All it needed was a new frame to attach to, a knob, and a dead bolt.

Through the thin walls, he heard the shower turn on. Veronica was naked. He gritted his teeth.

Make that two dead bolts.

Chapter Five

Matt had left like he'd said, ostensibly to get the first-aid supplies, but mostly because he needed distance to remind himself of all the reasons he wasn't attracted to her. The minute he returned and she opened the screen door, his rationalizations disappeared. She was wearing sneakers, calf-length pants, and an aqua silk shirt. She would have looked pretty wearing a garbage bag. And now here she was: dirt-free and wearing silk, of all things.

Her smile faded, and the screen wobbled. "You didn't have to come back. I'm sure you want to return to the job."

"I said I'd do this for you." He made an effort to stop ogling as he put his hand on the door and let himself in. "I want to."

Matt took a step and stared in shock. The countertops were white. The window was clear, and the trailer looked almost bright. He took another step to set down his first-aid supplies and realized that his boots lifted without sticking to the floor.

"How much did you pay your maid service to come down here and fix this place up?" As soon as he said the words, he wished he could take them back. The joke fell flat and made him sound like he was getting in another dig about her rich-girl life. Instead, he was amazed at how she — or anyone — had been able to make the place clean enough to pass a sanitary inspection.

"Enough that I can't afford to pay you to be my home nurse." Her voice was stiff. "I'll apply my own Band-Aids."

"Sorry." He rested his hand on her shoulder to convey his sincerity. He felt like he couldn't speak a full sentence in front of her without needing to apologize. If she could read his thoughts since he'd brought her back to the trailer, he'd have even more to apologize for.

Her hair spilled over the back of his hand as she turned and looked at him. It was as soft and silky as he'd imagined. "Sit down. Let me see your hands."

She braced her left hand on the table as she started to sit and then flinched.

Matt snatched it up and hissed out a breath. She was stronger than he'd given her credit for, but her body wasn't invincible, evidenced by her red, angry blisters. He picked up a tube of antibiotic cream and prepared to squeeze out the entire contents on her abused skin. He knelt on the floor beside her and looked her in the eye. "I am so sorry I didn't give you a pair of gloves."

"Are you really?" Veronica raised an eyebrow.

"Yes. I'm groveling on my knees."

She looked less than impressed with his efforts. "I thought your whole point was to push me over the edge, so I'll run back to my parents and spend the rest of my life sheltered and pampered, never coming within a fifty-mile radius of your town again."

"That…may have been my original plan. Yet you're still here, and I'm apologizing. Maybe you can help me figure out where I went wrong." He had pushed Kimberly over the edge—not intentionally, but he'd definitely thrown more at her than she could handle until she'd run back to the safety of her old life. He wasn't entirely joking in his plea to understand why it hadn't worked on Veronica.

Her lips quirked in a half smile. "This is the first job I've had where the people I worked with didn't treat me with kid gloves or give me fluff projects because of who I'm related to. I know you didn't intend for me to like you more because of the hard work I've had to endure, but I do."

He slathered on the antibiotic cream, trying not to dwell on how much he liked her, too. "So this is a little experiment into how the other half lives. Are you planning to go back to your old life when the novelty of being treated like a normal person wears off?"

"There's no going back." Her tone was serious. "I made a clean break. I left my credit cards, checking account, *everything* with my parents when I walked away Tuesday morning."

After watching her pull shingles, he could imagine how determined she'd looked when she made that choice. Kimberly never would have turned her back on her cushy life.

He let his fingers linger on Veronica's left hand for a moment longer than necessary before he released it and stood up. He wanted to step outside to give himself some space again, but he settled for sitting across the table from her before he reached for her other hand. "They're your parents. They'll take you back."

"I don't want them to, not if I have to agree to their conditions. I'm living life on my terms now."

He flipped her hand over and winced at the damage. Veronica had blisters to match those on her left hand, along with a raw scrape across the palm. She also had a deep scratch going down her thumb that he hadn't noticed when he inspected it on the roof.

She hadn't breathed a word of complaint.

"What kind of conditions?" He raised his gaze to her beautiful, flawless face. Whatever it was had to be bad if she was putting up with this much pain without a single tear.

She shook her head. "Marrying someone I've never been on an actual date with, who doesn't care I exist, just so he and my father can merge their businesses together. Besides all the backward notions about needing a marriage to seal a merger, the merger's not right for either of their businesses."

Matt's hand tightened around hers. "You came here to get away from your boyfriend?"

She rolled her eyes. "There's no boyfriend. You've touched me more today than he ever has. You're also hurting my hand right now."

He immediately relaxed his hold and focused on the job he was supposed to do. He had no reason to be jealous. Clearly, the other guy was a schmuck. Matt kept his fingers gentle as he applied the antibiotic cream. "How could you work with these kinds of scrapes?"

"That's what you were waiting for, wasn't it? For me to whine that I broke a nail? My manicurist is likely to faint when I come home to repair my cuticles—right?"

"A certified nurse could faint over these scratches. I think you should go to the clinic and have a doctor take a look at them." The over-the-counter antibiotic cream he was using might not be enough to prevent an infection. And if it wasn't, he was solely to blame.

· · ·

Veronica took over and finished securing the gauze. "I don't need to go to the clinic. I'm going to finish out my day working in your office."

"I suppose you could try to find my computer or shred some papers or something," Matt said.

Veronica sighed. Minutes ago he'd held her hands so tenderly she'd wanted to crawl on his lap and let him hold her. His soulful eyes had promised if there were any way for him to take away her pain, he'd do it in an instant.

But then he had made comments to remind her that he didn't see value in anything she could offer his business and she ought to go marry Mr. Always-in-a-Meeting-Leave-a-Message-With-My-Assistant. "Office work can be productive and beneficial to your bottom line, you know."

Hands properly bandaged, she walked out of the trailer to start the real, productive work of her day. She stopped in the middle of the gravel drive and looked around for her ancient, ugly car. Darn. She'd left it at the construction office when she'd ridden to the roofing job with Matt.

The screen door slammed, and Matt's boots pounded down the path behind her. "You've proven you can be productive against all the odds. I'll drive you to the office and show you the files for accounts receivable and payable."

She turned slowly. "I'm sure I'll find them, as soon as I unearth the computer enough to turn it on."

"I meant paper files. I don't actually use the computer for anything."

"Nothing?" Oh boy. He might not know it yet—and he certainly wouldn't believe her if she tried to convince him—but he needed her. A lot.

She smiled brightly. "I would love for you to show me your files."

Matt's brown eyes widened.

Her cheeks felt hot. That was much more suggestive than she had meant for it to sound. Not that she wouldn't mind checking out his, um, files.

"It's a deal." Matt offered his hand to her.

She accepted the handshake, steeling herself not to flinch with the anticipated squeeze to her abused flesh, but although he shook firmly, he didn't apply an ounce of painful pressure.

His gaze met hers then, and the connection stirred her all the way to her toes. This was too powerful to be labeled a deal. It was something more, something bigger…something she wasn't ready for.

Matt released her and strode to his truck. By the time she regained her equilibrium, he was sitting in the front seat waiting for her. "Ready?" he asked when she got in. He wouldn't meet her gaze as he cranked up the radio.

Ready to wow him with her business skills? Absolutely. She was going to do more than shuffle papers. She intended to put her biggest asset—her brain—to work for him.

Matt parked in front of the construction office and hissed out a word of frustration as he cut the engine. "Your grand file tour will have to wait. My not-so-silent partner has decided to speak up." His lips quirked. "You better not have a sister he's throwing at me this time."

"I'm an only child." Veronica followed his gaze out the windshield. Ron stood at the front door of the office, ramrod straight, his cane at his side, his gaze on her. "What do you think he wants?"

"Since you came to town, I haven't been able to make heads or tails of what he's thinking." Matt left the truck and crossed the small gravel lot.

Veronica pulled the door handle gingerly and followed him.

"You don't look like you've been working," Ron accused her when she'd closed half the distance between them.

She kept her head up and refused to let his words

discourage her, considering how hard she'd worked and how disastrous the results had been. "I started early, so I've already cleaned up."

"Working a half day counts as half a day, not a full day." He jabbed his cane into the ground for emphasis.

"Don't worry. My day is just getting started." She planned to wrestle the archaic filing system into oblivion.

Ron shifted his gaze to Matt. "I've decided I want a gazebo in my backyard."

"Okay," he said, as if the change of subject and random request were completely ordinary. "That's doable."

"I want it ready for this weekend."

"That's a problem." Matt closed the remaining distance between himself and Ron. "Everyone's tied up on the roofing job today. There's a seventy percent chance of rain tonight, so we need to get it shingled."

"You can build the gazebo tomorrow," Ron said.

"You should know it's not that simple. I have enough wood for the posts, but we'll need to set them in the ground with concrete before we build the rest of the structure. I'll also need to get more wood for the floor and sides. What do you need a gazebo for?"

"To enjoy my backyard and to have something that my granddaughter personally crafted. *She* can set the posts tomorrow. You can get the rest of the supplies over the weekend, so she can finish it on Monday."

"You want me to build you a gazebo?" As far as personal requests went, Veronica was certain it was the most bizarre one she'd ever received. With the success rate she'd had on jobs so far, Ron wasn't going to get much enjoyment out of her handiwork.

She hoped her book had a gazebo chapter.

"Veronica's not doing manual labor until Monday. Her

hands need a break." Matt lifted her wrist.

With the thick gauze surrounding her hand, she felt like she'd just been declared the winner of a boxing match.

"If she wants to run my company, she needs to prove she can suck it up," Ron said.

"She spent all morning sucking it up after I failed to provide her with gloves," Matt shot back.

Veronica's wrist tingled and her pulse throbbed where his fingers pressed against her flesh. She'd worked hard to earn his respect, and him standing up for her proved she was making progress.

Ron dismissed Matt and pointed his finger at her. "I expect you to set posts with concrete tomorrow or go home. Your mother must be frantic with worry about you."

Veronica had come to town envisioning Ron as a fairy godfather who was the answer to her dreams. Instead of embarking on an idyllic grandfather-granddaughter relationship, he'd ignored her and thrown her to the mercy of an unsympathetic town. Now two days later, he'd come looking for her because he wanted her to build something they all knew she was unqualified to do.

She didn't need Matt to defend her; the only way she'd make real progress was by fighting her own battles. She slid her hand from his grasp and rested her gauze-covered palm on his forearm instead, as she focused on Ron. "My mother knows where I am, and if she's worried, her concerns are unfounded. I'll go down to the store right now and buy those gloves so I'm prepared. I can't wait to build my first gazebo."

Ron's eyes narrowed on her hand. "Did you come here to work or to pick out a husband?"

She snatched back her hand, burned by the heat from Matt's arm as much as her grandfather's words. Matt was supposed to be a means to her goal, not a distraction. "I've been working as hard as I can to prove myself to you."

"If your mother knows where you are, why hasn't she come here to rescue you?"

Veronica gritted her teeth. "Because I'm not a little girl, and I can do my own rescuing."

"Really? I thought you e-mailed me to rescue you from your evil father's plot."

"He's not evil, and I e-mailed looking for advice. I appreciate that you went beyond advice to offer me an alternative, and I intend to make the most of it." Her heart hurt far more than her abused hands and feet. Why was it so hard for her family to accept her on her own merits?

Veronica drove the few blocks downtown. The hardware store was directly next to the grocery store. With any luck they would have an ample supply of work gloves in her size.

Despite her misgivings about Officer O'Malley waiting to bust her, she parked in the same spot from two days ago. She'd taped up her broken taillight the best she could until she'd earned enough money to pay for a replacement. She'd done nothing wrong. The townspeople needed to accept her. She wasn't going to hide from them.

The Hollisters were sitting on the bench outside the store again. Wilbur was dressed in yellow striped pants and a red plaid shirt. Agatha was wearing tweed slacks and a gray-blue velvet top. Veronica stepped out of the car and walked toward them. "Good morning."

"You're still here?" the mayor demanded.

"As a matter of fact, I am." Buying work gloves could wait a few minutes longer. She walked to the bench and sat in the small space between him and the edge. She could feel the surprise and hostility radiating from him, but she knew she had to try. If she could get the mayor to accept her—no guarantee by any means—she was certain the entire town would follow. "I've heard some disturbing rumors about this community, and I've been thinking, who better than the mayor to clear them up?"

"I don't weigh in on rumors," he said stiffly.

Veronica patted his hand. "I understand. After all, you've a savvy politician. And you obviously care about Kortville more than anyone. I've heard talk that you were promised money for a library building and baseball lights and a food pantry. I've also heard talk that because I came to town, you won't get money for any of those things because they were all contingent on the sale of Ron's distribution center. Which means it's in your best interest to get rid of me, so the sale can go through."

"You catch on fast." His tone was hardly complimentary.

"Now, Wilbur," Agatha began in reproach.

"Not fast enough," Veronica assured him. "I never dreamed when I was invited here that I'd be taking something that had already been promised. To be honest with you, I'm not sure that Ron wants it to go to me, either. Maybe you can help me understand where his heart and his intentions lie."

"His heart shriveled when your grandmother passed away," Wilbur said. "Most everyone says it died completely when your mother left home."

"Maybe having you here is bringing it back to life," Agatha suggested.

If it was, Veronica certainly hadn't seen any sign of it. But maybe Ron was just a lonely old man who'd tried to reach out but didn't quite know how to do it. Maybe asking her to build a gazebo was his twisted way of trying to connect again.

"So what's the worst that will happen if we don't get funds,

Wilbur?" Agatha asked. "The library can go for another year with bad plumbing. If they tear down that trailer, the baseball diamond will still be a go, and the teams can play during daylight hours without the need for lights."

"We can't let families go for another winter with no shoes or winter coats or go hungry when times are rough," Wilbur stated emphatically.

"Did you have time to read through that website?" Veronica asked. "Have you applied for any grants like they suggested?" Her grandfather should not hold the town's fate in his hands any more than her actions should have the power to take away their basic necessities.

"With the state budget in such a mess?" Wilbur snorted.

"Public money isn't the only option," she pointed out. "Some privately funded endowments and charities are set up to help with this exact kind of situation. I have contacts with a couple different groups that might be able to help you start a center." Groups she used to organize fund-raisers for. Organizations her parents thought were appropriate places to announce her engagement.

"What's in it for you?" Wilbur asked suspiciously.

Less traffic tickets on her record, buying groceries without being accused of fraud, walking out of the convenience store with something besides dusty doughnuts and melted ice cream, acceptance without needing to marry a well-connected man. "I get to prove that a city girl might have something to offer your town."

"We're not knocking city life," Wilbur said. "Matt went away to school and worked for a big engineering firm in Chicago before he gave it all up to return home."

"Why would he do that?" She'd left because she didn't have any opportunities anywhere else. But Wilbur made it sound like Matt had willingly turned his back on a successful career. She couldn't imagine him in a high-rise office. He was too physical and thrived on wide-open spaces. In fact, he didn't seem to like having an office at all.

"Because family matters to him and this town does, too," Agatha said. "Kortville Construction was his brother's company. Matt took over when Steve and Leah were killed in that awful accident out on County Line Road. Jenny needed him, and he needed this town to help him learn how to care for her."

"If you're going to tell her everything, don't stop there," Matt said. She hadn't heard him approach, but he was now standing in front of the bench, radiating a mix of horror, sadness, and fury.

• • •

Matt's chest squeezed, as it did every time someone mentioned "that awful accident out on County Line Road." Steve's death wasn't just a horrible tragedy. He'd been Matt's brother, his partner in crime when they'd pretended their house was haunted to scare little Becca Sanders next door, and the person Matt had called for advice when contemplating job offers.

He'd lost track of how many times he'd picked up the phone to ask Steve for advice, only to remember that Steve— who'd had so much to live for and who brightened everyone else's existence with his boundless energy—was gone. And Matt was on his own.

But if Matt was going to keep living, instead of burying himself alongside Steve, he couldn't accept pity—from Veronica or anyone else in town. "Tell her how my rich city girlfriend left me so fast she laid a patch of rubber from here to the interstate."

"That explains a lot." Veronica met his gaze, and to his relief, it wasn't dripping with sympathy. She pushed herself up from the bench without wincing at the pressure she placed on her injured hands. "But it doesn't have anything to do with the food pantry—actually, let's use a broader description, a community needs center—that we're trying to get off the ground. I'll make some calls and print out a few applications, and I'll get back to you, Wilbur."

The pressure on his chest subsided to a dull ache, knowing that she wasn't going to wrap her arms around him and smother him with condolences. "Did you go to the clinic yet?"

"I'm on my way to buy those gloves, and then I'm diving right into the office paperwork."

"The clinic?" Wilbur asked.

"I fought the roof, and the roof won," she quipped, waving a bandaged hand at him.

Matt begged to differ. She'd won. Her hands had battle scars, but she'd beaten his preconceived notions. Even Steve's hands-on wife Leah had preferred to leave the shingle work to her husband.

"You had her on a roof?" Wilbur demanded of Matt. "Did you at least give her some training and safety pointers before she went up there?"

"Don't worry. Matt was a great instructor," Veronica said, winking at him. "I'm just not the world's best roofer. I'm going to work in the office for the afternoon and let the guys do what they do best."

"He still should have taken better care of you," Wilbur grumbled.

"It's not his job to take care of me."

"No, Wilbur's right. I should have," Matt admitted.

"For goodness sake, that's the last thing I want," Veronica said in frustration.

"Well, he can at least help you pick out some appropriate gloves," Agatha said. Her gaze shifted to Matt. "And make sure she gets a canteen or a thermos, too."

"I'll make sure she has everything she needs before she works outside again," Matt assured her. He couldn't undo the damage he'd already caused, but he could ensure he held Veronica's safety in highest regard from here on out.

But Agatha wasn't finished. "You need to drink plenty of fluids, Veronica. Working out in the hot sun can dehydrate you fast. I'm worried that Ron and Matt aren't looking out for you like they should."

Veronica rolled her eyes but didn't attempt to interrupt Agatha, who was clearly on a roll.

"And goodness knows Toby can't even look out for himself, let alone anyone else. Do you hear he skipped school again today, Matt? Becca was fit to be tied when she got the call. I dare say that boy is more than she can handle."

So Toby *had* been skipping. Matt should have dug deeper when his gut told him Toby's story was fishy. "Is she still working in the grocery store? I need to let her know he was with me. I'll meet you in the hardware store," he said to Veronica.

"I'm coming with you." She leaned over and patted first Wilbur's, then Agatha's gnarled hands. "Thank you for taking care of me and looking out for everyone here. You're good people. The citizens of Kortville are lucky to have you representing them."

Matt strode away, but her words echoed in his head. Of course, he was grateful for everything the Hollisters and the rest of the town had done for him after Steve died. But when had he stopped to thank them? He gripped his cell phone, wishing he could dial Steve. He'd never needed his big brother's guidance more.

· · ·

By the time Veronica reached Matt and Becca, they were already deep in conversation, Becca's expression frustrated while Matt seemed to be reassuring her.

"I should have questioned his story more. It's completely my fault," Matt said.

"No. He needs to take responsibility for his actions. He can't lie to the adults in his life. He needs to concentrate on getting an education. How does he expect to have good enough grades to get into college if he keeps skipping high school?" Becca looked on the verge of tears. Her gaze landed on Veronica, and her face instantly stiffened.

"He's a great kid, really thoughtful," Veronica said. "You should be proud. His first concern was to offer me a pair of work gloves when I'd forgotten to bring my own."

"We'll get him through to the other side, Bec. The teen years don't last forever," Matt added.

Becca took a deep breath and dabbed at the corner of her eyes. "They certainly feel like it. Thanks, Matt. You, too, Veronica. You know…I've been thinking about your trailer. What you need are some flowers to spruce up your landscaping."

Veronica raised an eyebrow. "You mean, landscaping on the trailer that everyone's counting the days until it's torn down, with or without me inside it?"

Becca waved her hand, as if the detail was inconsequential. "You're going into the hardware store, now, right? Get the hanging baskets. Then you can take them with you."

"Right. Good idea."

Matt took her arm and steered her through the inside walkway to the hardware store. "You don't want to plant flowers," he muttered, once they were out of Becca's earshot.

She stared at the assortment of hanging baskets filled with colorful blooms and lush green leaves. No, she didn't want to plant flowers. But if she bought a dozen baskets, she could take Becca's suggestion and give her trailer a homey feel now, as well as take them with her when she moved into a permanent home.

She reached out to touch the one with pink-and-white flowers, and the price tag came into focus. She could not afford twelve of that price. She dropped her hand and looked around. On the wall behind her were dozens of seed packets that were—she finally understood the pun—dirt cheap.

Her hands throbbed at the thought of all the digging she would have to do. Giving up access to her parents' money did have a definite downside.

She looked back at the pretty baskets. She'd get one, so she could have some flowers now, and three packets of seeds that she could plant once she was settled in a new place and hopefully no longer ached everywhere. Veronica reached for the metal wires that led up to the hanging hook for the plant and lifted it down.

A pot full of dirt was a lot heavier than she anticipated. Her raw, scraped flesh screamed in protest as the metal wires dug into the gauze on her palm and fingers. She sucked in her breath as tears sprang to her eyes. She needed Becca to see her walking out of the store knowing Veronica had taken her advice. Her acceptance in this community required her to be mentally tougher than her soft, formerly pampered skin.

Matt lifted the planter out of her hand. "Don't touch anything," he ordered gruffly. "Tell me what else you want."

She blindly grabbed a few seed packets. Her hands trembled too much to offer to take back the flowerpot. What she wanted was to lean against Matt and soak up his strength.

"Agatha says you're the gloves expert, so you better help me pick out a good pair. I guess I need to defer to your expertise on a canteen, too."

"I'll fix you up." He brushed his index finger over an errant tear across her cheek. "Just don't cry, okay?"

He turned and walked down an aisle. By the time she wiped her eyes and took a few shuddering breaths to compose herself, Matt had picked out an insulated water jug and a pair of leather work gloves. He pulled a smaller pair of aqua cloth gloves with rubber grips on the fingers off the rack. "Were you just sucking up, or are you really going to garden? Because you need these if you are."

"I'm not allowed to do both at once?"

He swung toward her, the golden flecks in his eyes glittering. "This town is my family. If you hurt them, you'll answer to me."

His tenderness from earlier had vanished, replaced by a ferocious protectiveness that made her smile. Understanding why his loyalty ran so deep made her want to share in the town's bond even more. "I'm not hurting anyone. The people of Kortville matter to me."

Okay, so they hadn't rolled out a welcome mat for her. But the truth was, this tight-knit town *did* matter. The way they closed ranks made her want to be part of that wall of solidarity. Of course, before that could happen, she had to convince them she wasn't their enemy.

Matt set the flowerpot, thermos, and gloves on the counter and reached for his wallet.

No way. She might need to watch her budget, but she had to keep a closer watch over her independence. She set down the seed packets and covered his wrist with her hand. "This is my bill. I'll pay it. You can vouch for the authenticity of my money."

"I've always wanted to nail a counterfeiter." The female clerk's adoring gaze centered on Matt. If he wanted to cause Veronica more humiliation, this woman would be more than happy to accommodate.

Matt pulled his hand free and stepped back. "She's good."

Veronica let out a long, slow breath. As far as public acceptance, it wasn't much. But her insides warmed with hope. For the second time in an hour, he'd stood up for her, first to her grandfather and now here.

That warmth chilled immediately. Was she making progress, or had she merely traded her dependence on her parents for dependence on Matt?

Chapter Six

The irony of what she was doing wasn't lost on Veronica. To keep from marrying a well-connected man, she needed to use his connections with the Help the Less Fortunate organization to achieve her goal of breaking away from him. But she was willing to do it to prove to Matt and his town that she was committed to them.

Paige answered Trevor's phone. "Thanks for calling me back."

After the message this morning, Veronica should have known Paige would assume that was why she was calling. "I suppose Trevor's unavailable in a meeting."

"As usual," Paige said cheerfully.

"I called to ask him about his work with Help the Less Fortunate," Veronica said. The one thing that allowed their non-relationship to progress to the point of engagement had been his passion for this charity. While she'd focused solely on the fund-raising side, he'd left his precious meetings long enough to help people on the other end. "I have a town that desperately wants to provide food and clothing for its in-need residents, but it doesn't have the initial funding to get the plan off the ground."

"Would you like me to e-mail you the application, or are you looking for Trevor to wield some influence to get the town or state to cough up the money?" Paige asked.

"No offense to Trevor, but the mayor and I don't think any influence is going to get us money when there's none to spare." But how to delicately say that she wanted more than an application? To say she wanted special treatment wasn't exactly the truth; she was confident Kortville's application would be accepted on its merits. But if someone set it on a desk like the one in the construction office that she was wading through right now, it might not be discovered for years.

"Tell you what, why don't you e-mail me the completed application, and I'll personally hand it to Trevor. He'll be relieved to know you left to do charity work and not because you were trying to stop the merger. Everything can go on as planned now. He'll be happy to support your charity."

Veronica glanced at her bandaged hands. "I care about this charity, but that's not why I'm here. I'm getting my hands dirty working construction and living in a trailer."

Paige laughed. "I e-mailed you the application. Send it back as soon as you can."

Veronica started to protest that she was serious, but Paige had already hung up on her.

• • •

Matt had never wanted to regain total control of his company more than he did that morning. A rush job with no prior planning was bad enough, but this one also had the customer calling the shots because he thought a 50 percent ownership stake meant he knew something about construction. Consequently, Matt couldn't put the work on hold until he'd done enough preplanning to ensure the quality would be up to Kortville Construction's standards.

However, he could work day and night to make sure the most taxing physical labor would be done before Veronica arrived, and she could give Ron the appearance that she'd done everything. Last night with the rain soaking them, he and Toby had measured where the posts would go. The rain had stopped by the time he'd come back this morning to dig the postholes in the mud. The holes done, he returned to his truck for the posts.

Matt stopped cold at the corner of the house. Veronica was at the end of the driveway, wearing gloves, a T-shirt in her signature pink color, and designer jeans. Ron stood over her, directing her to mix three bags of dry concrete and water in the wheelbarrow Matt had spent the better part of an hour bending back into shape. Her stupid how-to book was open on the ground. She shifted over to refer to it.

"Now you need to push the wheelbarrow around the house to the gazebo spot," Ron ordered.

She straightened her shoulders and sucked in her breath. How had Matt ever thought this woman was a quitter? She didn't give up and didn't back down. But he couldn't let her push the wheelbarrow. Yes, she was wearing gloves, but the wounds on her palms couldn't take that kind of pressure.

"If we need a second batch of concrete, we'll mix it right by the holes," Matt said, walking down the driveway. "No need to push that heavy wheelbarrow through the wet yard if we don't have to."

She swung toward him, surprise and that same mix of vulnerability and determination on her face that she'd sucker punched him with at the hardware store yesterday.

"Leave it here until I set the posts in place," he continued. "Then I'll bring it to the backyard, and you can scrape the concrete out while I tip the bucket." He moved quickly to his truck to start carrying the posts. He couldn't take back what Ron had already done, but he could stop Veronica from injuring herself more.

"You don't have time to wait," Ron argued. "If you don't get that quick-drying mixture poured in the holes in time, the concrete will dry in your wheelbarrow. You won't be able to use it, and you'll have a heck of a time cleaning the equipment."

"It can wait," Matt said with authority. He hefted a post on each shoulder. As he headed around the side of the house, he had the pleasure of seeing Veronica's eyes slide appreciatively over his straining biceps. Just like that, every ounce of effort was worthwhile.

He set each post in a hole and turned around. Ron was marching toward him, glaring furiously. The sexual chemistry buzzing between Matt and Veronica was too thick. Was Ron finally stepping up to defend his granddaughter from Matt's baser thoughts?

"You want her gone or not?" Ron demanded.

That wasn't much of a defense. And Matt didn't know how to answer the question anymore, either. He didn't like what would happen to his town if she stayed, but she wasn't the spoiled snob he'd assumed when she'd first rolled in. "Normal manual labor is tough enough on her. You don't need to dream up ways to make it more challenging."

"You're welcome to get your heart broken again," Ron said. "But my daughter already broke mine when she left home and never returned thirty years ago. I did everything I could to get her back. I'm not letting Veronica worm her way into my heart until I have a guarantee that she won't run off like her mother did."

"Guarantees are hard to come by. Three years ago I'd

have sworn up and down there was no way I'd ever raise a little girl alone in the town I grew up in and couldn't wait to leave," Matt said. "But now there's no place I'd rather be."

"I'm sure Veronica would rather be somewhere else right now." As if to punctuate Ron's comment, she staggered into view pushing the wheelbarrow around the side of the house. She hadn't waited.

Ron put his hand on Matt's arm to stop him from running across the yard to her. "You came back and did us all proud. My daughter never came back. She was too good for me."

"So, you're going to punish your granddaughter?" Matt yanked his arm free and jogged toward Veronica and the load that was too heavy for her.

"No," Ron shouted after him. "I'm going to send her back to her mother, so she doesn't break Angela's heart the way Angela broke mine."

"Set it down," Matt called to Veronica. The ground was soft, making the single wheel dig in instead of rolling over the grass. "I'll take it the rest of the way."

"I've got it," she wheezed. "This is construction, not a tea party, remember? I'm supposed to work, not sit around and let you wait on me."

"I changed my mind." Regardless of the hell Ron would give him for it, he couldn't watch her fail, not with the guilt eating at him for how much her hands had to be killing her.

"You want to wait on me?" She looked up from her load, and the anticipation in her gaze tempted him to haul her in his arms and kiss her eyelids and lips until she forgot everything that had ever given her a moment's pain.

Before he could reach her, though, the wheelbarrow's front wheel hit a muddy divot. Veronica stumbled, and the tub tipped. Her arms twisted as she tried to balance the equipment, but she didn't have the strength to muscle it upright. The wheelbarrow turned on its side, taking her down, too. Her shoulder gouged into the mud. Her hip banged against the metal tub. Concrete poured out onto her leg and the grass.

Matt's heart sank. This was his fault—he should have stood up to his heartless partner sooner. No matter how much she wanted to foolishly ignore her limitations, she didn't deserve this. He pushed the wheelbarrow aside while she struggled to sit up.

"I have cement shoes." She wrestled herself to her feet. "You could dump me in the river. No one will ever know."

"I'm not going to dump you in the river. It's ten miles from here." He strove to match her light tone, but he couldn't laugh—not when he'd treated her so progressively worse with each job that the possibility he'd stoop that low sounded almost believable.

"Well, gosh, that's comforting."

He managed a grin this time at her sarcasm.

"We won't dump you in the river. We'll send you home to your mother!" Ron shouted. "I'm going inside to find out why she's not here yet. Use the outdoor faucet to clean up. Your mother won't want that mess inside her car."

"Yet?" Veronica asked, bewildered. "What does my mother have to do with anything?"

Ron slammed the back door in reply.

She turned to Matt. "Does concrete wash off, or did I permanently gain fifty pounds?"

He brushed his thumb over the mud on her cheek. "It washes off, but you're not going to like it. You'll have to hose down your clothes. If you don't want to strip, we'll have to do it with you in them."

Her blue eyes widened in horror. "Hose down my clothes? You're joking, right? Is this one of your industry terms that translates to 'build a two-story gazebo with six birdhouses in the backyard and have it done by noon'?"

"I wish." He wanted that hot appreciation back in her gaze when she looked at him, not this humor.

Veronica closed her eyes and sank to her knees. "Ron hates me. I thought he was the first person to ever believe in me, but he wants to see me fail more than anyone."

Matt kept his hands steady on her arms and lifted her to her feet. Right now, he would do anything to erase the defeat on her face. He wanted the woman back who believed no obstacle was too big to overcome. "I don't think his motives have anything to do with you. He still seems fixated on the fact that your mother broke his heart when she left home."

"Don't attempt to convince me he has a heart." Her voice took on a hard edge Matt hadn't heard before. "If he treated my mother this way, it's no wonder she hasn't spoken to him for my entire life."

Matt swallowed. "How about we make a deal? I won't try to convince you if you don't let his bitterness taint you."

She studied him for a moment. He could feel her resolve strengthen as she held up her weight instead of relying on his hands. "You've got a deal, with these conditions. I'll hose myself down. Then I'm going back to the trailer and crawling under the covers. I'm going to start this whole day over again; I don't care who's supposed to be the boss. *I'll* decide what job I'm going to spend my day on."

The woman of steel determination was back. Veronica marched to the faucet and twisted the knob. The hose jerked and rippled with the hard stream of water pumping through it. She picked up the nozzle and pointed it at her shoes. The water splattered up to her face.

She flinched but moved the hose higher up her legs. "Oh my gosh, this is cold. So cold, and it stings. Is there a temperature adjustment?"

"It's an outdoor faucet," Matt reminded her. "Cold is the only option."

Propriety demanded he look away. But as the water hit her body and splashed in every direction, it drenched her pale pink shirt. Matt wasn't a testosterone-laden teenager hoping for a wet T-shirt contest, but his body reacted like he was.

Veronica shivered so much that she dropped the hose, shooting water over the muddy grass and onto his boots. She made no move to pick it up and finish rinsing.

"Your left side is still completely covered." He didn't want this job. Right now, he'd give up his half of Kortville Construction to wrap her in a towel and warm her abused flesh, instead of doing what he had to do. Grimly, he picked up the hose and pointed it at her.

The concrete slowly came off, thanks to his merciless pounding. He'd rather turn the hose on himself—maybe it would cool his own body down.

"So this is how the Kortville Mafia takes care of its victims. Next time give me the cement shoes and throw me in the river." She should have looked like a drowned rat. Instead the water sparkled off her in the sun, and she looked like a glorious water queen.

He flicked off the nozzle. "Is all the residue gone?"

Concrete was drying in the wheelbarrow and the grass, empty postholes littered the yard, a muddy river flowed next to the faucet. But all Matt could think about was taking Veronica in his arms and burrowing under her covers with her.

"How would I know? I can't feel my skin." She shivered uncontrollably, which took away from her royalty but not her sparkle, as she peeled off her gloves.

"Your hands are bleeding." The evidence stained the wet

gauze. He set the hose down and gave in to his need to hold her. "I'm sorry. This is my fault. I take complete responsibility."

She tucked her hands behind her back and stepped away from his embrace. "You're responsible for my klutzy walking and astounding ability to lose control of a wheelbarrow?"

"Veronica." He reached for her hand. "Please." He needed her to let him touch her, not just to ease his thick wad of guilt, but because he was a man who took care of and protected others. He needed her to give him another chance to do that.

Her gaze warmed as soon as he said please, and she stopped moving. "I'm not really going to spend the day under the covers. I'm taking an early lunch hour. Then I'll go to the office to put in the rest of my time. All I need is a little favor from you."

"Anything." He closed the distance between them again and settled his hand on the small of her back.

Her breath slid in and out shakily. He'd like to think it was from his touch, but his ego wasn't that overblown. The morning's ordeal was the only thing on her mind. "Explain to Ron that you're doing the job without me. I'm not returning to his house."

She was not, however, stomping back to Chicago, either, vowing never to set foot in his town again. Ron might be immune to her grit and charm, but Matt wasn't. He stepped closer and brought the hand that wasn't resting on her back up to brush a drip of water from her cheek.

"Take the next two days off, along with the rest of today. Kortville Construction doesn't work on Saturdays or Sundays, unless there's an emergency. Go with your plan to crawl under the covers for the rest of the day."

"There aren't enough blankets in the trailer to get rid of this chill." Her eyes focused on his lips. She was battered and soaked, all but begging him to warm her up.

There was nothing Matt wanted more. If they were going to start something, he wanted to be the one taking the initiative, not following blindly.

He pressed his mouth to hers. Her lips were cold, but soft and sweet, and they warmed instantly to his touch. He cupped his hand against her wet cheek. She shivered in response, her breath steamy and shaky against his mouth.

Matt released her and stepped back. He had no choice. His body was nanoseconds from shaking, just like hers, and he didn't have the excuse of being freezing cold. He rubbed his hand over his face, praying it wasn't trembling.

Everything he tried with her spiraled out of control.

• • •

In two short hours, with an astonishing amount of stupidity, Veronica had managed to ram her independence completely into the ground. She'd failed to hold up her end of the workload—literally. Not only had she turned the job into a slapstick disaster, she'd let Matt hose her down like a piece of machinery, and then acted so needy he kissed her.

Ron was waiting for her at the front of the house, leaning on his cane with obvious disapproval. "Your mother is on her way here to take you home."

Her skin was bruised and icy, her muscles aching, and her pride raw. But it was frustration that finally got the best of her. "I'm not going anywhere. I don't know why you keep bringing her up. You and I had a deal that has nothing to do with her, and I intend to honor it. Are you going back on your word?"

"Of course not. You're the one who can't—"

"Good. Then call my mother, and tell her you made a mistake. I'm already home."

With her head held high, she walked to her car parked in

the street. She couldn't stop her eyes from stinging, but she turned her head away so he wouldn't notice.

Matt bounded out of Ron's house with a big blue blanket over his arm.

She wished she'd left before he could join her. She needed so badly to be alone, where she could sort through her humiliation and craving for Matt.

"Wrap this around you." He set the blanket, which turned out to be a hand-knitted afghan, around her shoulders. "Get in the truck. I'll drive you to your trailer."

She hugged its warmth to her chest, willing her teeth to stop chattering. "I'm not leaving my car here. He'll have it towed."

"I'll make sure he doesn't." Matt kept his gaze steady on her, even when Ron snorted rudely. "In the past three days, you've nearly fallen off a roof, passed out in the grass, and swam in concrete. Not to mention your hands are the consistency of raw hamburger and your feet probably aren't much better. You're not in any condition to drive."

The only reason her driving ability was in question was because the kiss had rattled her reactions and senses beyond comprehension. But if Matt hadn't already guessed the truth, she still had enough pride left to keep it to herself.

"I'm not out to ruin your job. I'm well aware physical labor is my weakness. No one is more eager than I am to work in the office where I can capitalize on my strengths. When my month is up, I will leave Kortville Construction in better condition than it was when I came, and you can thank me then." She marched to her car.

"You have to contribute something to make things better. You haven't done anything that proves you have anything to offer," Ron called, limping down the driveway toward her. "And don't you dare leave with that blanket, or I'll call Connor

O'Malley and report you for theft. Your grandmother knitted that herself."

Veronica folded the blanket and marched back, setting it in his arms. Then she returned to her car, turned the ignition—letting it grind for a full minute before it finally caught—and backed out of the driveway.

As she drove to her trailer, her mind raced. Staying at a job site she had no qualifications for wouldn't prove anything except that Ron was right. Well, she wasn't going to let him and Matt blow off her real skills the way her parents had.

Trevor had blown her off, too, in favor of his many meetings and business contacts that were always a higher priority than her. She had a lot to offer, both personally and professionally. It was time she took action and made a man see that, instead of letting him lead the relationship in the direction he wanted it to go.

Speaking of men, she realized Matt was following her in his truck. Her Olds crunched over the gravel in the trailer park and stopped in front of her trailer. As he pulled in directly behind her and got out of his truck, she stepped out of the car and squared her shoulders.

"I know you probably want some time alone," he said. "But I want you to think about this."

She tried not to shiver. If he'd decided he had something important enough to say that he followed her across town, it couldn't be good news.

"I know you have good intentions," Matt continued gently. "But Kortville Construction doesn't need you. The distribution center doesn't need you. You're better off taking your strengths somewhere that appreciates them."

Well, now she knew the direction he wanted her to go—straight out of town and down the interstate. "Really? You don't appreciate my strengths? *You* don't need me?" She sauntered to him, not stopping until her body was flush with his. "So, then can you tell me you don't need this?"

She pressed her lips to his. This time she was taking the initiative. She'd decide how fast and far she wanted to go, and she'd decide when she had enough and end it. Except her control melted as her body brushed his hard muscles and her mouth molded against his soft lips. The delicious, sweet taste of him consumed her.

She disentangled her limbs from Matt, horrified that she hadn't taken control of anything. She'd simply been carried away by instinct and desire. Her only saving grave was that Matt's glazed eyes and swollen lips proved he'd been swept up as much as she had.

She wanted so much more than she could ever have, and right now none of it had anything to do with career plans and independence.

Veronica showered and changed, the one thing she excelled at in the construction business. She was also at the end of her stack of clean clothes. She would have to check out the Laundromat that evening. But first, she needed to go into the Kortville Construction office. She'd found her way around the place yesterday. Now she was going to make her mark on it.

She walked outside to her car and grimaced. She was finally dry, but the driver's seat was soaked from the short drive to the trailer. She should have kept Ron's blanket and taken her chances with the police.

She squared her shoulders. A wet seat was a minor inconvenience compared to the aches and pains of muscles she never knew she had and which were now threatening to immobilize her. She wouldn't crumple, no matter how close to the edge she felt.

She went back inside to get a towel. She covered the seat in the car, so she wouldn't soak her last clean pair of pants on the way to the office. She'd had enough of wearing wet clothes for the day.

"I thought I had the wrong address in my navigation system. You can't possibly live here."

Veronica looked up and whacked her head on the top of the car frame. Her mother was stepping out of her luxury Mercedes, teetering in her stilettos on the uneven gravel.

If Veronica had looked half as ridiculous and out of place when she'd first driven into town, it was no wonder the townspeople had scorned her. Of course, most of their opinions hadn't changed, so it was likely she still stood out like a sore thumb. She rubbed her tender scalp. "You couldn't possibly have made the trip in less than an hour."

"Of course not. My father, after not speaking to me for goodness knows how many years, called me last night and told me you're here and you wanted me to pick you up."

Ron had called her last night. He had planned for Veronica to fail with the concrete work from the beginning, and she'd been so stubbornly determined to prove she could do it that she'd walked right into the humiliation. But he'd misjudged her. She wasn't grateful for her mother's rescue.

"Your father is delighted, not to mention Trevor," Mother continued. "He would have come himself, of course, but he had a pressing meeting."

Of course.

Whoever married Trevor would probably have to go through the ceremony with his personal assistant because he'd be in a meeting. "Mother, Ron has manipulated both of us. I have no intention of leaving."

"Of leaving what? That shack you're standing in front of?

Darling, please don't tell me that heap of metal between us is your new car. If Trevor saw the way you were living, he'd drop you like a hot potato."

"We're not together, so there's nothing for him to drop."

"Don't be ridiculous, honey. He couldn't get out of his meeting, but he's willing to send his secretary down to talk to you. You can't let her see this shack."

For all of Matt's frustration with her, he'd never discounted her as a person. He didn't tell her she was ridiculous when he iced her thumb or hosed concrete off her jeans. He never sent Toby or his other employees to deal with her, so he wouldn't be inconvenienced. "I'm sorry if my home embarrasses you, but I didn't invite you or your friends *or* my non-fiancé's personal assistant here for a dinner party, so how I live shouldn't concern you at all."

Mother shifted on her precarious footing and picked her way slowly across the gravel. "Is there a place other than that trash heap"—she glanced at the trailer and shuddered—"where we can sit and talk?"

"Tonight I'm washing my clothes at the Laundromat; you could sit with me there. But I can't talk right now. I need to go into work. You should have called to see what I wanted before you made the trip to take me away from a life I have no intention of leaving." She wouldn't walk away from it for anything her parents could give her. But she hoped her mother didn't question her motives too closely, because she was no longer sure if her career plans or Matt were keeping her here.

Mother looked confused and hurt. "I don't understand. We've always given you everything you needed, so you wouldn't have to live like this. I know we argued before you left, but it's time to put that behind us. Come home, Veronica, darling. I'm sorry we didn't pay for your school for you. We'll pay off those silly loans now, if you'll come home and set a wedding date with Trevor."

Veronica knew her mother truly didn't understand. She really thought she'd done all the right things. She probably thought she'd done Veronica a favor by steering her life so she'd never have to work for a living. "I already paid off my loans, but even if I hadn't, businesses can merge without a marriage alliance to seal the deal. I won't be part of the payment. Do you have any idea how insulting that is? I could help both companies make their businesses better if they would listen to me. I have skills, Mother."

"I have skills, too, I'll have you know," she replied, clearly affronted.

"I know you do." Veronica touched her mother's arm, desperately wanting to find a way to reconcile without giving in on the issue that was dividing them. "I admire your charity work. I'm in awe of the way you can pull off a dinner for fifty people in two hours and make it look like every detail had been fussed over for months. But I don't want to plan dinner parties for Trevor."

"What do you want?" Mother asked.

"I want more than just a guy. I want a fulfilling career and a home of my own." She'd come to Kortville to get away from men and stand on her own two feet. Yet right now she couldn't claim to have come close to accomplishing either objective.

"I see. It's all about you. Your father was depending on you to wield influence from the inside, as only family can do, but you don't care if he gets pushed out of the company he built from the ground up when Trevor takes over." Mother spun on her toes and nearly fell in the loose gravel. Gingerly, she made her way back to her car. "I tried so hard to instill you with unselfishness. Clearly I didn't do as good a job raising you as I thought." She slammed the door and reversed into the street without checking for traffic.

Gravel dust settled over Veronica's boots. Her blisters throbbed. Her grandfather was against her. Her mother was against her. She'd failed to help her father when he needed her most.

She had wanted to make a life of her own. Now she truly was on her own.

Chapter Seven

With each keystroke, another sliver of excitement and anticipation replaced Veronica's depressed mood. She understood the construction business a hundred times better from sitting alone in a neglected office entering bills and invoices into the slow, outdated computer than when she'd studied her *Do-It-Yourself Home Improvement Manual* and attempted the actual work.

No doubt some people would consider that another knock against her. But as the afternoon wore on and the financial picture became clearer, it reinforced her confidence in her strengths.

"Darling, you are never going to believe what your grandfather tried to do."

Veronica looked up as her mother walked into the building, leaving the door wide open behind her. She was sure Mother would have been, if not all the way home by now, certainly back in her own neighborhood. Instead she was limping in her stilettos and looked close to tears.

Veronica pushed away from the paperwork and pulled out a chair, guiding her mother to sit down. "What's wrong?"

Instead of sitting with her normal perfect posture, Mother slumped against the armrest. "I went to see Daddy. He invited me inside, sweet as you please, and then locked the door and went on a tirade about how disappointed he was that I hadn't returned home in thirty years. He had the nerve to say I was grounded, and then while he was yelling he had my car towed right out of his driveway."

"Why would he tow your car?" A fly buzzed through the office. Veronica walked to the front door and closed it.

"So I wouldn't have any way to leave the house and get back to my husband. As if that isn't enough, I left my purse and phone inside the car, so I can't even call anyone to tell them my father turned into a lunatic and was holding me hostage."

Veronica dug out her cell. "Would you like me to straighten it out for you, or do you want to?"

Mother snatched the phone. "I'm calling for a limo, and I want it filled with Godiva and champagne. When I leave town, I'll have the driver go nice and slow by Daddy's house, and I'm going to roll down the window and stick my tongue out at him."

Veronica resisted rolling her eyes. Saying anything to get in the middle of their feud would only bring her down to their level. "So he didn't call you to pick me up. He called you so he could punish you for leaving home decades ago?"

"He lives alone in that house and hasn't changed a thing since my mother died. Even my bedroom is the same as the day I left. It's creepy."

"Maybe he's just really lonely and misses you and Grandmother, and this was the only thing he could think of to bring you back," Veronica suggested, wishing she'd pushed harder when Ron had refused to let her inside his house on that first day. She'd been too busy focusing on her own needs to consider his.

A set of car doors slammed outside, and the entrance to the office opened again. Veronica expected Ron to have tracked his daughter down. Instead, a woman she didn't know held the door, and Matt's niece came inside.

"Hi." Jenny smiled. "Is Uncle Matt here?"

"No, he's still at this morning's job, I think." Veronica smiled back, pleased to see the sweet girl she'd met at the diner a few days ago.

The other woman frowned as she stepped in behind Jenny. "He knew I had to drop her off early today. I'm Glenda, Jenny's babysitter. I'm also in charge of the town picnic tomorrow, and I've got to get the grills ready, or we'll be stuck eating raw hamburgers."

"Town picnic?" Veronica vaguely remembered seeing some sort of flyers hanging on the door to the diner. But no one had said anything to her about it. She'd been so preoccupied that an upcoming town event hadn't registered.

"Yes, it's a potluck, but burgers and hot dogs are provided. Tickets are five dollars each." She reached into her purse and pulled out a packet, mostly of stubs. "We're raising money for the new baseball field. Your grandfather's donating the trailer park land, but we have to bring in dirt and sod, and then we need money to maintain it. We're hoping to have it ready in time for some of the adult softball league games this summer and all of the high school's fall baseball season."

"I'd love to buy a ticket." Veronica forced herself to maintain her friendly smile, uncomfortably aware that she was living over home plate and her trailer was the first thing that had to go to fulfill their plan. "Mother, why don't you spend the night with me while we sort this out? You can come, too."

"I'd rather spend the night in my old bedroom than in

that awful trailer," she said.

"I'm sure Ron would love that." Veronica pulled a ten out of her purse and exchanged it for two tickets. "Jenny can stay here until Matt comes back. I'll let him know you stopped by."

"Oh, that would be so wonderful," Glenda gushed. "Jenny, is that okay with you, honey?"

"Yes, Miss Veronica and I are friends."

"Oh, thank you so much," she said to Veronica. "I'm swamped with this project. I had no idea what I was getting into when I volunteered to be manager of the summer athletics program this year. You are so nice. Barney was completely wrong about you." She rushed out the door before Veronica could question her about what Barney had said.

She turned to Jenny and smiled. "It's good to see you again. This is my mom."

"Nice to meet you, Mrs. Jamison," Jenny said, holding out her hand formally.

Mother shook her hand and smiled. "Nice to meet you, too. You have impeccable manners. Your parents have taught you well."

"My mom and dad died, so my uncle taught me," she said matter-of-factly.

Good manners and a hard-luck story—her mother was putty. Remembering the tortured look on Matt's face when he'd overheard the Hollisters explaining his brother's accident and his desperation to change the subject, Veronica felt like putty herself.

She busied herself with picking up the picnic tickets to put away for tomorrow. *Bring a dish to pass* was written on the bottom of each one, and she realized she could use some motherly advice. "Mother, what do people bring to a potluck?"

• • •

Matt was repairing the damage to Ron's yard when his cell phone rang. He checked the caller ID: Veronica. He was so freaked out by the kiss—kisses—they'd shared that he almost let it go to voice mail. But he wouldn't allow her to think their encounter unsettled him to the point that he was avoiding her.

"I'm working in the office, and I wanted to let you know that Jenny's here with me." Veronica's sweet, cheerful voice flowed over him, momentarily stunning him into silence with memories of all the reasons he was attracted to her.

"Jenny's with you?" The last thing he'd expected her to call about was his niece. "What happened to Glenda? Why didn't she call me?"

"Apparently you had a prior arrangement with her that she was going to drop Jenny off here, and you're the one who didn't show."

"Oh shoot, is it after four already?" He pulled back his phone to check the time. The gazebo disaster had taken much longer to rectify than he had anticipated.

"Four thirty, but it's okay," Veronica said in a voice clearly meant to soothe him. "My mother's here, too, so they're entertaining each other while I'm tracking down her car."

"Your mother?" Jenny had talked of nothing but Veronica ever since they'd left the diner two days ago—her hair, her clothes, her shoes, her smile, her makeup. It was no wonder Matt was fixated on her after being subjected to glowing reviews on every feature. And now Jenny was going to subject him to a double dose.

"Ron called my mother just like he'd threatened. But apparently, his goal isn't to send me home but to convince my mother she needs to move back in with him. His method of convincing her is to tow away her means of transportation. I'm working through the bureaucracy at the police station to get it sorted out."

"I'll be right there," Matt said.

"Jenny's fine," Veronica repeated. "You don't need to rush over. I'm just letting you know where she is."

In his office with Veronica and her mother, one of whom she barely knew, the other who was a complete stranger. He tossed the mostly clean wheelbarrow in the bed of his pickup, dialed Connor's direct line, and headed for the office.

By the time he arrived, he had Connor's assurance that the confiscated vehicle would be released and returned immediately. Veronica was sitting at Leah's desk inside the office. She'd unearthed a section all the way down to bare wood and had the computer up and running. He doubted he could make her understand that paying bills by hand was faster and cheaper than keying in everything, categorizing, and still having to write the checks manually.

Jenny sat on a cushioned reception chair using another cleaned-off section of the desk to carefully print her spelling sentences from her homework. In theory, it was the perfect scenario. Jenny would have her homework done, so they wouldn't have to labor through it together that weekend. Veronica would waste her time fiddling with a computer system he didn't use, instead of messing with something essential to his business.

In the perfect situation, Jenny wouldn't be wearing a dozen necklaces and bracelets and rings on every finger. He took a step closer. She didn't have on cheap costume jewelry, either. "Where did you get all that?"

Jenny looked up, and her face brightened into a smile. "Hi, Uncle Matt."

Veronica looked at him, her gaze thoughtful.

"I got here as soon as I could," he said to Jenny. "Pack it up, and we'll go home."

Her smile faded. "After I finish my homework, Veronica promised she'd braid my hair the way that girl on TV had hers last night."

Letting her watch a mere five minutes of a televised teen pop star's concert had been a bad idea. He'd allowed it. Now he was responsible for undoing the damage before her girlie tendencies turned her as self-centered and superficial as Kimberly. "I'm sorry. Your plans will have to change. We're going home now."

"Matt, if you have work to do, I don't mind," Veronica finally spoke. "We're getting along fine."

"I'm done for the day. Give the jewelry back, Jenny." He couldn't help remembering that Veronica's love of pretty things hadn't turned her self-centered or superficial. He'd stereotyped her based on her looks, the same way he'd assumed she would look down her nose at him and his town.

"Oh, do you have to leave so soon?" A woman in a skirt and high heels came out of the bathroom down the hall. She looked like an older, more sophisticated version of Veronica. Her gaze shifted from Jenny to him. "So, you're the man in this equation. I knew there had to be one somewhere."

"Oh, Mother, for goodness sake," Veronica said, but he didn't miss that her cheeks turned pink. He liked the fantasy that he was important enough to affect her plans. "The only equation he's made a difference in is that he knows how to pull the right strings in this town. Your car, complete with your purse and a gift certificate to the diner for your troubles, should be in front of the office in fifteen minutes."

Matt tugged on the neckline of his T-shirt. That was the only thing he'd made a difference in? Those kisses earlier didn't count for anything? After she'd turned his life upside down and inside out?

"What are your intentions toward my daughter?" Mrs. Jamison demanded, not missing a beat.

"His intentions are to put up with me for a month until I've earned the right to run the distribution company," Veronica answered, clearly trying to deflect the pressure, even as her cheeks turned brighter by the second. Okay, maybe she was thinking of those kisses more than she wanted him to know.

He looked back at Mrs. Jamison and had the sinking feeling that her gaze hadn't wavered from him as he'd ogled her daughter. Ron might have been blinded by his own agenda to Matt's raging hormones and inappropriate thoughts, but Mrs. Jamison clearly was not.

"Jenny, I need a stapler. I think there's one in the conference room. Would you mind getting it for me?" Veronica asked his niece.

Jenny looked at him for permission, and he nodded. This was no conversation for a little girl to be party to. Veronica might have been affected by their kisses, but her brain was working a lot better than his to protect Jenny without making her suspect anything out of the ordinary.

He waited for his niece to leave before answering lightly, "I've done everything I can to send Veronica back to you."

"Have you?" Mrs. Jamison drilled him with frosty blue eyes. "What do you mean by *everything*?"

Okay, he hadn't done *everything*. If Veronica knew half the things he imagined, she'd run back home as fast as her clunker car would take her. If her mother knew, she'd likely use her connections to have Matt locked up so fast he'd never see another minute of daylight as long as he lived.

"Not *that*, Mother." Veronica sounded appalled. She stood and touched her mom's arm. "Like you, Matt believes that I never should have left the comfort of your home or stepped foot in this town."

"Does he?" Mrs. Jamison said coolly. "I'll have you know, Veronica was raised to be a lady and to have high standards when it came to men."

And Matt came up short. He'd tried to be a society man before, and it wasn't for him. But it scared him how much he'd been willing to consider trying again when his arms were locked around her and her soft lips were pressed to his.

"Matt and I have a business relationship," Veronica said firmly. "Nothing more. I'm in Kortville because it's part of my career plan, not because a man is keeping me here."

A statement like that begged for Matt to revisit those kisses from earlier and make himself the reason she was sticking around. He wouldn't pretend to have long-term intentions. A lasting relationship between a debutante and a construction worker was never going to happen. If his experience with Kimberly wasn't enough of a reminder, Veronica's mother looked plenty eager to set him straight on how much of a chance he had with her daughter.

• • •

"What are your intentions toward our Matt?"

"I beg your pardon?" Veronica balanced the laundry basket against her hip, trying to close the trunk of her car with one hand.

Becca stood by the Laundromat door, her own basket tucked against her hip, looking considerably less friendly than when she'd offered Veronica landscaping tips for her trailer earlier. "Everyone's talking about you two sucking face until he couldn't see straight."

Veronica managed to close the trunk, but her basket slid to the ground, dumping a pair of pink lacy panties on the pavement. Now her underwear was on display for the entire town to see. Could she not preserve an ounce of pride?

"You saw us kissing?" Much more intriguing was the thought of Matt so affected by the kiss that he couldn't see straight.

"Not personally. But Barney burned a whole batch of doughnuts while he was staring through the window. Rumor has it he has a really good pair of binoculars under his cash register. He doesn't miss a thing that goes on across the street."

"I-I see." She understood now—and not just about the spy network that she'd clearly underestimated. Deflecting questions from parents and society matrons trying to protect her was practically second nature for Veronica. But no one had ever been concerned that *she* might break a man's heart, give him a bad reputation, or otherwise be a bad influence. She'd always been the good girl. Mostly, it was her upbringing, but no one had rendered her incoherent with attraction to make her want to break the rules, either.

She doubted the townspeople would take comfort in knowing she was in uncharted territory. She certainly couldn't. She already depended on Matt to help her navigate the construction business. She couldn't let him have control over her emotions, too.

"I don't have any intentions, except to be a good neighbor and employee and to plant a few flowers so my trailer doesn't look like it was dropped on a post-apocalyptic landscape."

Becca snickered as she pulled open the Laundromat door, gesturing Veronica inside ahead of her. "You know, I have a lot of good neighbors, but they don't go smacking their lips on mine." She sighed. "Not that I don't fantasize about it once in a while."

"Yeah? Anyone in particular you're fantasizing about?" Veronica asked.

Becca's cheeks turned pink, and she dumped her basket on an empty counter, giving the sorting process more concentration than it warranted. "At this point, I'd fantasize about anyone with a pulse."

Veronica laughed, not believing her for a second. "Surely you have better prospects than that."

Becca slanted her a look. "You trying raising a sixteen-year-old truant and having a life of your own to boot. Getting back to my point, though—the whole town is looking out for Matt. We've seen how you rich girls dazzle him and how much you hurt him when you leave."

It seemed Matt had given up *everything* when he'd come back to take over his brother's life. To Becca and the others who lived here, Veronica was no different than the woman who hadn't been strong enough to give him what he needed. She set her basket in the opposite corner and crossed the room to Becca, touching her sleeve earnestly. "You don't have to worry about me hurting Matt. Whatever physical contact people witnessed, it had nothing to do with a relationship; nobody's going to lose their heart. We both have more sense than that."

At least she knew Matt did. She was no longer certain about herself.

• • •

"Uncle Matt, if you can't do braids, can you twist my hair like this?"

Matt glanced at the ripped-out magazine page Jenny held up. The starlet posing for the camera had an overteased, oversprayed mop of orange hair. "Where did you get this?"

"Stephanie brought it to school. She said her mom is going to fix her hair like this for the picnic tomorrow."

He set the picture facedown on the coffee table. "Why don't we cut yours short so you don't have to worry about fixing it at all?"

"No." She leaned her head back, making her shoulder-length mane reach the middle of her back. "I like it long. Can I call Veronica to style it for me?"

He swiped his hand across his lips, which still tingled with the memory of Veronica's mouth pressed to his. "No. We're not going anywhere tonight, so all we need to do is comb it before you go to bed."

"But I want to do something fun. I looked everywhere, and we don't even have pink bandanas."

"Bring me a brush and two ponytail holders, and I'll give you pigtails. Then how about we go outside and play some catch." Whatever Veronica's Friday night plans were, he was sure they were more exciting than throwing a ball around. But Matt was perfectly content with the low-key entertainment.

Jenny made a face. "Pigtails are for babies. When can I see Veronica again? She likes dresses and pretty hair. She even has that song we listened to on TV on her iPod."

Matt rubbed his temples. Despite his efforts, he couldn't mold his niece's personality into that of a tomboy. He hated the wistfulness in her voice when she talked about the things he was denying her, as if he were standing between her and happiness. "What about Stephanie?"

Jenny's eyes brightened, and she snatched the magazine page off the table. "Can I call her and see if she can sleep over tonight? Pleeeease."

A sleepover full of girl talk, pop music, hair spray, and makeup. He'd rather vacate the house and pitch a tent in the yard. "What about playing catch?"

"I want to play with Stephanie."

He couldn't keep denying Jenny. She was already trying

to latch onto Veronica to fill the void he was ignoring. He needed to give her acceptable outlets, preferably under his supervision. "All right, you can call. No sleepover tonight, though. She can come play for a couple hours, and we'll take her home before bedtime."

Jenny went into the kitchen to retrieve the phone. A couple minutes later, she returned with her hand over the mouthpiece. "Can I go to Stephanie's house instead, and then sleep over at her house next Saturday night?"

"Let me talk to her mom." Matt held out his hand for the receiver. Heidi was a practical small-town single mom who was having a tough time making ends meet. She wouldn't fill Jenny's head with frivolous nonsense. But that did nothing to thaw the icy fear gripping him that this little girl who was his final connection to his brother could grow up into a sophisticated, superficial woman. A woman who had nothing but disdain for him and the path he'd chosen.

• • •

"So I'm confused," Veronica said, taking a five-dollar bill to the change machine. "Is Toby your son? You can't possibly be old enough—"

"No, no. Brother. Although really, if you ask him, I'm probably just the maid who does his laundry."

"What about your parents?" Veronica asked. The machine spit the bill back at her. She flattened it and fed it in again.

"Long, boring story. Look at these jeans." She held up a pair that were caked in mud and no doubt belonged to Toby. "I'm so thankful he loves doing construction and working for Matt, but honestly I've never seen clothes so disgustingly dirty as what comes off him after he gets home at the end of the day."

Veronica smiled genuinely despite the blatant change of subject. The machine rejected her money for the third straight time. "What's the trick to get this quarter machine to take my bills?"

Becca looked up from stuffing her brother's clothes in the washer. "Ignore what it says. It won't take fives. Only ones."

"Oh." Veronica took back her five as the machine spit it out once again. At least it wasn't targeting her for fraudulent currency. "I don't have singles. How do I get change?"

Becca glanced at her watch. "The grocery store's closed. You'll have to go to the diner. Pauline will switch it out for you."

Veronica laughed. She couldn't help it. "How many espressos will I have to drink before she gets around to it?"

Becca looked confused for a moment, but then her eyes brightened. "Here's what you do. Say, 'Pauline, I want the daily special to go, and I need change for the Laundromat because you know those damn dryers are going to eat every quarter I have and I'm going to be there all night as it is, so I need to run.'"

"The dryers take that long to dry the clothes?" Veronica asked. She'd hoped to make it back to her trailer for an early night.

"If you're lucky. If not, be prepared to wear damp clothes for the next couple days."

Veronica resigned herself to the change of plans. At least she would be in good company. "How about I get two specials when I make the diner run? It sounds like we'll be making a night of it."

Becca grinned. "Sounds heavenly. I can't tell you the last time I've hung out on a Friday night with someone I'm not related to."

"As a bonus, I have a pulse, too," Veronica said, and they

both dissolved into laughter.

. . .

Matt took the screen door off its hinges and leaned it against the trailer. Veronica likely wouldn't be pleased if she came back and found she had no door. But he'd promised he would fix it on his first free evening, and he planned to not only have the screen back on but the repaired front door hung before she came home. He'd be long gone, too.

He tried not to think about where she'd disappeared to. She wasn't alone in her trailer, and she sure hadn't made an effort to spend the evening with him. He forced himself to block any more speculation. After he fixed the door, he needed to swing by the office and see whether she'd trashed his filing system. He hadn't paid a bill or sent an invoice all week. Work took priority over a fantasy date with a woman who never would have given him the time of day if she hadn't been forced into close constant contact with him.

"Is this part of the business relationship you have with my daughter?" someone demanded.

Matt turned to find Veronica's mother walking across the gravel toward him. He hadn't heard her drive up. She'd gotten her car back, and apparently, it was as quiet as it was expensive. She was wearing the same freezing stare she'd turned on him earlier. Only this time Veronica wasn't here to deflect her, and Jenny wasn't around to soften her gaze.

Matt squared his shoulders and prepared for frostbite. "This is being neighborly. You might not recall what it's like here, but in Kortville we look out for each other, and everyone pitches in to help."

Her mouth tightened. "What happened to the door that made it need to be replaced?"

Provoking her wasn't a prudent idea, but Matt, hick that he was, couldn't resist. "I broke it trying to convince her she was better off with you."

"You forced your way in on her?" Mrs. Jamison reached into her purse—for a gun, Mace, or a cell phone to call the police, Matt wasn't sure which, but he valued his life enough to explain.

"No, no. I broke it trying to convince her the trailer wasn't in livable condition and she shouldn't move in here. She moved in anyway."

Mrs. Jamison studied the tacky trailer. "I don't understand what possessed her to do this. She's always been such a good girl. I hate to blackmail her, but she has to understand her father could lose everything without her cooperation."

"Cooperation with what?"

"The merger. Her life, her family, her fiancé are in Chicago waiting for her to get over her jitters."

"Her fiancé?" Matt repeated. Veronica had mentioned not wanting to marry some shmuck, but a guy who didn't care if she existed wouldn't be her fiancé.

She didn't kiss like a woman who had a man she loved waiting for her.

"Does he love Veronica?"

"Everyone loves Veronica," her mother said confidently. "Anyway, what's Kortville Construction worth?"

"To me—priceless. Why?" Matt turned back to hanging the door, hoping she'd take the hint that she'd overstepped her bounds, not shoot him in the back.

"I need a dollar amount. If you don't know, I'll pay for the appraisal. I'll deposit a check for exactly half the amount in your personal account and you can use it to buy out my father. My only condition is that you immediately fire Veronica."

Matt carefully leaned the wooden door against the trailer

again. Veronica would be furious if she ever found out. "You want me to fire your daughter so she'll come home and marry some guy who'll then merge his company with yours?"

"It's the only way my husband can keep himself involved in his company once the businesses are combined," Mrs. Jamison said, twisting her hands on her purse handle.

"You've certainly done your research to figure out what I want," Matt said. "Have you ever asked Veronica what she wants?"

He hadn't asked her, either. But when they kissed, he hadn't had to. He knew.

Chapter Eight

After she and Becca had recovered from their fit of laughter, Veronica settled in her car to make the quick trip from the Laundromat to the diner. She'd just managed to get the engine to turn over when her phone rang. Her heart lurched, but when she looked at the screen, disappointment hit her hard. "Hi, Paige."

"Trevor can get you the funding for the community needs center," she said briskly.

Veronica had e-mailed the application back less than an hour ago. She hadn't expected a response until at least next week. "In exchange for?"

"Your appearance with him at your father's board of directors' dinner party tomorrow night. He needs to show that the engagement is on to get your father on board for the merger."

If she did it, she'd give up all her principles that had led her to leave home in the first place. If she didn't, she'd never get the townspeople to accept her and carve out the life she wanted here. "Was this my parents' idea or Trevor's?"

"All I know is it wasn't my idea." Paige sounded perturbed.

"Where's the funding coming from?"

"I'm e-mailing you all the details. You can think about it tonight, and I'll send a car to get you tomorrow afternoon."

"I have a car," Veronica replied. This wasn't how she had planned things. Helping the town was supposed to help her, too. Now getting Kortville's inhabitants to accept her meant sacrificing her future here.

She wrapped up the conversation, parked in front of the diner, and mentally repeated Becca's speech. Then she pasted a smile on her face and walked past the flyers for the picnic and into the building.

"Oh, Veronica, you have to try this strawberry-mango chilled espresso," Pauline called from behind the counter.

She was tempted to agree. Pauline's passion for her concoctions was contagious, but the night was already turning into a much more demanding project than she'd anticipated. "I need two specials as a carry-out, and I need a bunch of change. I'm doing laundry, and I'm told the dryers are going to take all night, so I need to get back to them."

"Those dryers *are* awful, aren't they?" Pauline said with feeling. "I wish we could organize a boycott of the Laundromat. You have to come here for quarters, the washers start smoking if you overload them by so much as a single sock, and you could stay there for three weeks and the dryers will never get the clothes totally dry."

Veronica wished she'd researched her clothes-washing options before she'd committed to using the Laundromat. She'd have to check with Becca to make sure she hadn't overloaded the washer. She did not want her clothes to start smoking. "Who owns it? Have you told them your concerns?"

"Wilbur and Agatha." Pauline rolled her eyes. "Look, they're good people, but they have a washing machine in their house. They don't understand how frustrating it is."

The Hollisters were the most approachable people in town. If there was a problem, no one wanted to create a solution more than they did. "They care about the good of the community. Maybe they never realized the dryers don't work."

Pauline looked as though she didn't believe it for a second. "I hear you're trying to help them out with the food pantry and clothing drop off they've been talking about for years. If you earn their eternal gratitude by setting one up, see if you can get them to repay you by upgrading their washers and dryers."

"You have a deal." Veronica smiled for real this time. "Can you add two strawberry-mango espressos to our order so Becca and I will stay awake while we're drying our clothes?"

Pauline beamed at her as the door to the diner opened again. "I'm experimenting with sushi, too. Let me send some and a rating packet with you."

Oh no, she knew better than to get sucked into rating anything. "Just the specials and the drinks and a lot of quarters tonight. If I'm going to taste test, I need to give it my full concentration, and we both know I won't be able to do that in the Laundromat."

"You have sushi here?" a woman asked from the doorway.

Veronica turned around. Her mother had stepped into the diner, her gift certificate in hand.

"I do, but I'll need your opinion on whether it's as good as what you're used to in the city," Pauline said, giving her new customer her full, delighted attention.

"Um, Mother, Jenny would recommend you get a grilled cheese if she were here."

"I'm sure that's a lovely choice for an eight-year-old." Mother paused. "Are you going back to your trailer?"

"No, I'm washing my clothes at the Laundromat.

Apparently, the dryers take quite a long time."

Mother shocked her by giving a satisfied nod. "Good. The longer the better." With that she walked to the counter, dismissing her. "Now, are you Pauline? Tell me about your sushi."

Veronica took her food package and hustled out of the diner. Back in the Laundromat, she gave Becca one of the Styrofoam containers, which turned out to be fried chicken, and put a round of quarters in the washer.

"What is this drink?" Becca asked. "It isn't half bad."

"Strawberry-mango chilled espresso." Veronica gave her best Pauline imitation. "Now by 'not half bad,' do you mean you'd rate it a seven or a ten point two?"

Becca laughed.

Veronica dropped into the chair next to her. "Pauline thinks if I can help the Hollisters get the community needs center set up, I'll be able to convince them to replace the appliances in here. What do you think?"

"Replace the washers and dryers? I wouldn't bet on it, but have you seen the empty backroom?" Becca set down her chicken breast and walked over to push open a scratched door tucked away in the corner. "The location is absolutely perfect, and they wouldn't have to beg Ron for a big wad of dough for a new building."

Veronica followed her into the room as she considered Paige's offer again, which led her to thinking about her grandfather's promises. "If enough people believe there's a need—"

"There's a need," Becca assured her, "and it deserves a better solution than Wilbur and Agatha giving away their clothes so all they have left are the items that no one of any age would be caught dead wearing."

"Then we can organize the community to come together

to fill it." Anticipation, rivaling the thrill of Matt's hand cupping her arm, rolled through Veronica. Unlike with the construction business, she'd been thoroughly trained by her mother on how to get the people and funding in place to pull a charity off the ground and give it momentum.

Her financial and business training had taught her what the organizations needed to become self-sufficient, too. If she convinced the townspeople to trust her, she could come up with a solution that didn't depend on marrying Trevor just to take advantage of his foundation's generosity.

Becca arched a brow. "We? Are you planning to stick around?"

"I've always planned to, despite everyone else's tactics to get rid of me."

"Yeah…about that," Becca began tentatively. "Sorry I caused that big scene in the grocery store and embarrassed you."

"It's all forgiven," Veronica assured her. She was already moving on to imagining this room filled with gently used jeans, new packages of underwear, and warm coats. How could she not let it happen, simply because the deal Paige had offered made her sick to her stomach?

Becca returned to the laundry room and checked her washing machine. "You have to understand how much Ron has offered to this town. His wife died and his daughter left him in the space of a month. The story goes it was only the bigheartedness of the people here that pulled him through."

Veronica reluctantly closed the door to the empty backroom. "What's the story on Matt?"

"That's easy. He needs to make enough money to buy back Ron's investment, so he can run the company the way his brother did."

So he didn't have to hire people like her. Becca didn't

have to say it. They both already knew.

"He's all about supporting the projects other people envision for the town. He'd like to donate free labor for all their causes."

"That's at odds with his goal of making money to buy out Ron."

Becca shrugged, as if there was no conflict. "He'll put the town first. He feels like he owes them that much. They were here for him when he needed them most. Aside from Jenny and honoring his brother's memory, giving back to the people who helped him is his number-one priority."

Veronica could either make that her priority, too, or prove that her mother was right when she said her daughter was just plain selfish.

Veronica stepped away from her car onto the grass. She stood for a moment surveying the bustling town park in the bright midday sunshine. To her right, children climbed through colorful plastic playground equipment, laughing and shouting.

Straight ahead, adults milled around a makeshift stage. Some were setting out hula hoops and jump ropes, but most stood chatting with one another. Everyone—adults and children—wore department store jeans or shorts, discount T-shirts, and sneakers or flip-flops.

Veronica rubbed her hand down the side of her black chiffon dress. "It's tasteful, elegant, and works for any occasion," Mother had assured her yesterday afternoon. And she—stupidly thinking her mother knew more about small-town life having grown up here—had taken her advice. Mother never missed the mark when it came to dressing appropriately for an occasion, so it didn't occur to her to get a second opinion from Becca.

She focused on the other side of the stage. Next to a cluster of picnic tables, a very hot construction worker tended to a smoking grill. Matt, of course, was part of the jeans-and-T-shirt crowd. And she had to admit, the outfit looked a lot better on him than anyone else. His white tee fit like a glove against his ripped chest. His jeans fit looser but were well worn, molding to his thighs and backside.

Not wanting him to catch her staring, she deliberately looked away from his tantalizing body and scanned the park for Wilbur. He was the mayor. Surely, he'd be dressed up.

The banker who'd been wearing a suit in the grocery store when he verified her fifty-dollar bill walked across the stage and tested the microphone to an eardrum blast of feedback. He wore a polo shirt, shorts, and Crocs.

On the other side of the playground, a man came shuffling down the sidewalk wearing green plaid pants and a collared shirt with navy-and-yellow stripes—Wilbur, dressed in his finest. Veronica pivoted to return to her trailer, her stiletto heel digging into the soft ground. She'd change clothes and return to the picnic before anyone noticed her gaffe.

"Veronica, you came!" Jenny dashed across the grass to her.

She'd been noticed.

Veronica smiled and opened her arms to give the girl a hug. "Of course I came. Your babysitter worked hard to make this day special."

"Uncle Matt's cooking burgers and hot dogs. Do you want one?" She pointed toward the grill.

This time Matt looked straight at her, his gaze traveling the length of her not-so-basic black outfit. Add to the long list of things he and the town would hold against her. She couldn't do much about anything else, unless she took Trevor's offer, but she could fix what she was wearing. She forced her gaze back to Jenny. "Maybe later. I'm going to dash home and change into jeans. I'm a little overdressed."

"No, I love your clothes." Jenny rubbed the chiffon skirt between two fingers. "My uncle won't even let me wear high heels."

"When you're older, I'm sure you'll get some," Veronica said gently. "They can be pretty hard to walk in." She lifted her heels out of the holes they'd created in the soft ground and walked gingerly to her car.

She'd return wearing jeans, a T-shirt, and sneakers and start working on the plan for the community needs center that she and Becca had come up with last night. She turned the key in the ignition. The engine ground an eerie sound. The noise was awful and completely wrong coming from a car.

People turned and looked toward the parking lot. Through the windshield, she could see several of them speaking to Matt, while gesturing toward her at the same time. He held the spatula in his hand but ignored the grill as he watched her, his mouth a flat line. Those hot kisses they'd shared yesterday clearly hadn't softened his feelings toward her.

Inside her car, every warning light on the dash was lit up—oil, engine, gas—giving her no clue what the real problem was. She opened the *Do-It-Yourself Home Improvement Manual* on the seat beside her, but it didn't have a chapter about fixing cars. The vehicle wasn't going to spring to life on its own, she didn't have a clue how to make it work, and she'd attracted everyone's attention.

She was stuck in her inappropriate black dress, so she'd have to make the most of it. While she was networking, she'd also check out who was a mechanic in town. She was either going to win over the townspeople today, or she would go down in a big, designer chiffon flame. Either way, she was guaranteed to get people talking.

. . .

Veronica's cleavage was monopolizing the bank president's attention. For the last twenty minutes, he'd practically drooled in it, periodically nodding his head so she'd think he was listening.

Matt was too far away to have any idea of what she was saying. If she was complaining about the ill treatment she'd received from the town, she could go on for hours on what had been said about her since she'd arrived looking gorgeous and out of place.

"She certainly keeps life interesting around here, doesn't she?" Connor O'Malley pushed his holster to the side as he propped his foot on a nearby picnic bench. "I'm disappointed I wasn't on patrol when you had her on a roof. Was she wearing that same dress?"

"No, thank God. Jeez, Connor, she worked her butt off on that roof."

"So I hear. For a whole fifteen minutes each day before she gets a blister or is too tired or dirty to continue," Connor scoffed.

Matt concentrated on shifting the burgers around the grill, so he wouldn't be tempted to smack Connor with the spatula. He'd harbored the same misconceptions when she'd first rolled into town, but it irritated him that anyone could still believe superficiality was part of her true personality. After spending a good part of the week demonstrating there wasn't any room in his company for a pampered princess, he knew she wasn't one. "Ask Toby. He'll tell you how hard she's been working."

"Toby." Connor sighed. "I heard he skipped school again.

That boy is going to land himself in serious trouble if he doesn't watch it."

"He's a good guy," Matt pointed out. "How many kids skip school so they can work instead?"

Connor shook his head. "His friends are trouble, and I worry about Becca. She's got her hands full already."

Something in Connor's tone made Matt take a second look at him. "Becca, huh?"

"By the way, Mrs. Parker's on my case to arrest you," Connor said, pointedly changing the subject. "Something about an overdue library book."

Ugh. If Mrs. Parker was that worked up about it, he wished she would go through with her threat to march over to his house and get the book herself. "What a terrible crime wave. You might need to bring in backup for this case."

"You're three weeks overdue. She *almost* has a case. Can you get her off my back and just return the damn thing?" Connor stared across the park.

Matt could smell the burgers burning, but he ignored the grill to follow Connor's gaze.

Veronica smiled at the balding banker and gave him an overdone two-handed shake.

"That's quite the friendly handshake," Connor said.

Matt's fingers squeezed around the spatula until his knuckles ached.

"Of course. I don't know why I didn't see it before."

"What?" Matt tried to wrench his gaze away from Veronica but couldn't. The banker held her hand long after any business handshake would have ended. If he didn't let go of her right now, Matt was going to march over and deck him.

Veronica pulled away and stepped back, depriving him of the opportunity. She sashayed away from the stage toward the parking lot.

"You've got it bad," Connor said. Before Matt could play dumb, Connor's attention was diverted to the parking lot. "Holy moly. Towing that Mercedes yesterday was the highlight of the decade for Fred. I didn't expect it to be around today."

Mrs. Jamison was back. Kortville Construction could have been all his if he'd taken her offer. Veronica might be on her way to the city to marry that other guy. All his problems would have been solved. But for some reason, he just hadn't been able to stomach the thought.

"Take over burger duty for a couple minutes." Matt tossed the metal flipper to Connor and strode across the lawn toward the parking lot, where Veronica was joining her mother.

Mrs. Jamison handed Veronica a platter. She looked at it, and her expression deflated. "Did you bring anything besides sushi?"

"Pauline and I spent five hours last night getting them exactly right. They are the best sushi rolls I have ever had," Mrs. Jamison declared.

Matt was right in front of them now. He'd eat every single burned hamburger if that platter wasn't crystal.

"We already stick out like the proverbial sore thumb. People are looking for a reason to resent us," Veronica said in a low voice.

Her sensitivity to the townspeople's opinion made him pause. He was as guilty as Connor for thinking she was too busy looking at them with condescension to notice anything else.

She shifted the crystal tray arranged with circles of sushi. "I trusted your judgment when I should have worn jeans and brought a Crock-Pot of baked beans. You might think you're doing me a favor, but all you're doing is pushing your daughter further away."

Matt couldn't stand still and listen to her heartbreak for

another second. "Hey." He stepped forward and reached out to put his arm around her waist. "Did you bring a dish to pass?"

"Apparently, we did." Veronica sidestepped his embrace and pasted on a smile. She did it so convincingly he wouldn't have known she felt out of place if he hadn't seen her expression moments before.

"I didn't do this because of you," Mrs. Jamison said. "I brought the sushi because Pauline worked hard on it. She's really proud of what she made, and I wanted to help her show it off. And that's your grandmother's crystal tray. Don't get me started on how long it took to convince Daddy to let me borrow it for the day."

Veronica smiled genuinely this time. "In that case, I think it's time we introduced Kortville to the culinary delight that is sushi."

Matt tried not to be like the banker and let his gaze drop below her smile. Unfortunately, allowing his eyes to feast on her full, sultry lips only made him want to kiss off every speck of her rosy-pink lipstick.

Oblivious to his thoughts, she waved Pauline over to join them. "My mother is giving your sushi rave reviews."

Pauline beamed. "Did you try one yet? Matt, have you tried it?"

"Believe it or not, I've had sushi before," he said. "It's not my thing."

Veronica picked up a seaweed-wrapped roll and popped it in her mouth. "Oh wow, Pauline, this is amazing. Mother, you were right. Perfect ten. Ron!" she called, waving him into their circle from the parking lot. "I love your wife's crystal tray. It's absolutely stunning. You have the perfect match for this delectable concoction Pauline came up with. Have you tried one of her sushi yet?"

Ron limped over, leaning on his cane, and reluctantly plucked a roll off the tray. He chewed for a moment, considering. "Not bad for something that belongs at the bottom of the ocean."

"I knew we'd make some converts," Veronica said, as if he'd also bestowed the delicacy with a perfect ten. She stood on tiptoe and brushed her lips across Ron's weathered cheek. "Come on, Pauline. Let's take these around to the tables and make sure everyone gets a bite." She walked away, the heels of her ridiculous, bewitching shoes sinking into the ground with each step.

"I thought the sushi would remind her of her favorite food and give her another reason to come home," Mrs. Jamison said, sounding flummoxed. "But she acts like small-town life agrees with her."

"A lot of people would say that you've come home, too, Angela," Ron pointed out.

"I might decide to visit on occasion if you would welcome me, but my home is in the city with my husband, Daddy."

"I thought…if I convinced you to come home, you'd want to stay."

Matt had never thought of Ron as an old man, but he certainly looked every one of his seventy-eight years as he twisted the end of his cane into the grass.

Mrs. Jamison simply rolled her eyes and turned to Matt. "Have you thought any more about my offer?"

"What offer?" Ron demanded.

"To take my money and buy you out, so he can fire Veronica. She and I have a dinner party in *our* hometown tonight. She has a man waiting to marry her, and her father needs her to make sure he doesn't get squeezed out of his own company in a merger."

"I'm not taking money from my daughter." Ron hitched

up his cane and slammed it down again. "I paid for you to go away to that fancy school so you could come back and run my distribution company, Angela, not marry some rich trust-fund pansy. You are not paying me with a cent of his money."

"He's a good person, Daddy. You never gave him a chance."

"If he's such a good person, why did Veronica come to me for help getting away from him?"

"Mrs. Jamison." Jenny skipped toward them. "Can you come see me on the playground? I can do a cool trick on the monkey bars. Come watch, please." She grabbed her hand and tugged.

"Jenny, leave Mrs. Jamison alone," Matt warned, reaching to peel his niece off the woman's expensive pant leg.

"I'm perfectly capable of telling people to leave me alone if they're bothering me," Mrs. Jamison informed him, shifting Jenny out of his reach. "This girl is not bothering me. You and Daddy, however, are getting on my last nerve."

She dismissed Matt and Ron with a flick of her head and took Jenny by the hand. "I'd love to see you on the monkey bars, honey. Did you know they were Veronica's favorite part of the playground when she was your age?"

"Really?" Jenny's words faded as she walked away, but the skip in her step remained.

Matt looked at Ron. He was leaning on his cane and staring after his daughter, his undisguised wistfulness and loneliness making him appear old and frail. He caught Matt looking at him and growled, "Wait until that niece of yours gets old enough to leave and ends up in some ritzy Chicago neighborhood where she's suddenly too good to come back and visit you. Then you'll know how I feel."

Matt knew Ron was trying to rile him up. Still, as he watched Jenny stare adoringly at Mrs. Jamison, he remembered how she'd gazed at Veronica with the same reverence and adoration. And Matt could all too easily imagine Ron's prediction coming true.

• • •

"Who would have guessed sushi would be the hit of the picnic?" Becca laughed as she helped herself to another one, but her expression quickly sobered. "You haven't run into Toby anywhere, have you?"

"No, but I'll keep my eyes peeled," Veronica promised. She looked over the park, but the only person who stood out was Matt, chatting with another family a few tables away.

"Want me to ask Connor to look for him?" Pauline asked.

"No," Becca said quickly, panic filling her face before she masked it. "I mean, no need to bother the police. Toby's around somewhere. Just tell him to check in with me if you see him."

"Sure thing," Veronica said, for now going along with Becca's desperation to play it cool.

Becca smiled a weak thanks and hurried off.

Pauline shook her head. "She's got her hands full with that brother of hers. And you have your hands full with that hideous car you've been driving. Have you met Fred yet?"

"Fred?"

"Agatha's cousin's son-in-law. He's the mechanic who's kept my car running for the past five years. I'll introduce you. He's at the picnic table on the far right, wearing the blue shirt and talking to Matt."

As if hearing his name, Matt looked up and caught her eye.

Veronica's cheeks heated, and she curled her toes as the tingling shot through her body. She said the first thing that came to mind to keep Pauline from suspecting how hard she was falling. "Those strawberry-mango chilled espressos you sent with dinner last night were divine. I love that you've figured out a way to offer gourmet options at diner prices."

The restaurant owner blew out a breath. "I haven't figured out anything. Every one of those darn things costs me more that I sell it for, and that's assuming I charge for it and don't offer it as a free tasting."

"You can't operate a business that way." Veronica's professional concern was instantly on red alert. For all of Matt's sloppy record-keeping, she hadn't seen any evidence that he was taking on jobs that cost him more than he charged. He simply needed to do a better job of collecting what he was owed and pulling profit out of services that people were willing to pay a premium for.

"Tell me about it. For years, I've been trying to figure out a way to keep the restaurant profitable while scaling back my own hours, and every year I'm working harder and longer for less. The only part I love is trying out new gourmet options."

They were almost to Matt and Fred's table. Veronica rushed to offer Pauline her services before they arrived and Matt could remind them both she already had a job—one she was intensely bad at. "This is going to sound totally dorky, but I love cranking out that kind of analysis. If you'll trust me with your financial books and long-term goals, I'll do it for fun."

Pauline eyed her suspiciously. "What's in it for you?"

"Sushi and strawberry-mango espressos, I hope." She tried to keep her voice light.

"Deal," Pauline proclaimed.

Veronica blinked. She'd half expected Pauline to sneer and trample her offer, but she hadn't. Maybe Veronica was starting to make progress. "Thank you."

"No. Thank *you*." Pauline smiled and turned to Fred. "This

is Veronica Jamison. She's the sad owner of the atrocious olive-green Oldsmobile that belongs in the demolition lot."

"Nice to meet you," Veronica said, holding out her hand to him. "Do you think there's any hope for my car?"

"Hope's what keeps me in business, honey," Fred said, accepting her handshake. "I'll take a look at it and see what I can do. Since you're Matt's girlfriend, I'll give you a special rate."

Matt's girlfriend. She looked at him to see if the words sounded as good and right to him as they did to her.

He had frozen in the process of turning away. "Better give her the full rate, Fred. We're not together."

She swallowed her disappointment. He was right; he already was in charge of too many decisions that could ultimately dictate her success or failure. She couldn't allow him to take control of her future happiness as well.

· · ·

Matt made his way back to the grill and relieved Connor of the spatula, vowing to concentrate on the burgers. But Veronica kicked off her shoes and started walking around barefoot in her designer dress. The next time he looked down, the meat was black.

He put another set of raw burgers on the grill, but Veronica's interactions with the townspeople sidetracked him again. Glenda clucked her tongue at him. "I've had several requests for Connor to come back and take over the grill," she said. "But I think we can call it a day when you finish that set. I'm going up on stage to announce the raffle winners."

The burgers were just about cooked to perfection when Glenda announced Veronica's name as a winner. She cheered with genuine excitement as she made her way to the stage to collect her raffle prize of an oversize Kortville baseball T-shirt. She held it up to show everyone and then slipped it over her head and wiggled it down over her dress.

"Thanks for helping me dress appropriately," Veronica said, giving Glenda a hug, the microphone picking up her words for everyone to hear. "Now I need to win some pants."

Matt guffawed and laughed along with the rest of the crowd as he watched her stroll back to the picnic tables. Instead of silently watching her walk by and whispering after she was gone, people reached out to talk with her. Veronica laughed and modeled her shirt for her new admirers, looking sexier than anyone had a right to look in a shapeless tee.

"I was wearing those shoes. Give them back," a girl shouted across the park.

"They're not yours."

Matt looked up as he recognized Jenny's voice. She was holding on to the heels of Veronica's black shoes and arguing with Stephanie, who was sporting a bizarre hairstyle of multiple pigtails and overteased bangs.

Matt looked around for someone to hand off the spatula to. Connor had disappeared, but it didn't matter. The once-perfect burgers had charred beyond recognition. He pushed the meat to the edge of the coals and left it there.

"Yes, they are. I found them." Stephanie pulled on the toes of the shoes as hard as Jenny pulled on her end.

"Girls, what are you fighting about?" Veronica asked, reaching the children before Matt could.

"These are *your* shoes. She's trying to take them," Jenny said, her face screwed up in an adorable tough-girl stance.

"They *were* my shoes," Veronica agreed with Jenny. She looked at Stephanie. "But I didn't take very good care of them, did I?"

Stephanie met her gaze and shook her head.

"If you had shoes like those, would you take good care of them?"

She nodded solemnly.

Matt stood still, not wanting to interrupt when she was handling the situation so well on her own.

"Then here's the deal." Veronica crouched in front of both girls. "You can have my shoes. I think they'll be great for playing dress-up. I bet you and Jenny could play with them together." She put her arm around Jenny, and his niece reluctantly released the footwear. "You know what else you girls need?"

Matt knew what he needed. He needed Veronica to put her arm around him and look at him with that same serious intensity. On second thought, he wouldn't be able to control his needs if she did.

"An awesome bracelet to go with the shoes." Veronica continued talking to the girls as she slid two thin silver bangles off her arm and handed one to each girl.

Stephanie accepted hers warily. "Do I have to give it back?"

"Definitely not. If you can take care of the shoes and bracelet better than I did, then they deserve to be with you forever."

The girl smiled at Veronica for the first time. "Thank you. Jenny and I are going to be the fanciest ladies ever." She clutched her new shoes to her chest and grabbed Jenny's hand. Their matching bracelets rattled as they ran off together.

Matt closed the distance as Veronica straightened, rubbing her knees where the soft ground had left damp imprints. "Why did you do that?" he asked.

"Let's see, because I have fifty other pairs of black shoes, because I prefer gold to silver, because I'm bribing the kid so her great-aunt will consider selling me that awesome farmhouse just outside of town, because I get off on flaunting my wealth. I'm sure you could come up with a laundry list of reasons."

She'd pegged him. He was guilty. She'd been proving him wrong and destroying his misconceptions from the beginning. Everyone else at this picnic had reversed their opinions of her. Although he was beginning to understand what Veronica wasn't, he still didn't know who she was. How could he comprehend what he could offer her if he couldn't figure out her motivation? "Why, Veronica?"

She shrugged, rippling her oversized shirt with her shoulders. He could too easily envision her climbing out of his bed and wearing one of his shirts as she padded around his house. "Because wearing those shoes made Stephanie happy."

"And your goal is to make people happy?"

"It certainly beats making them unhappy." She stepped toward him and lifted her hands to his shoulders. "What can I do to win you over?"

Matt looked her up and down. He couldn't admit that she already had. The more she focused her gaze on him and touched him, the deeper he was drawn in. "Another kiss would probably do the trick. But I'd settle for you coming to work on Monday wearing that T-shirt."

Chapter Nine

Veronica didn't kiss Matt, and she didn't make any foolish, flirty promises about what she'd be wearing come Monday morning. Not that she hadn't been tempted to do both.

The picnic was winding down. Her mother had long since left to prepare for the dinner party in the city, and Ron had disappeared about the same time.

Before Veronica could move forward with Matt, she needed to call Paige and tell her to cancel the application to the Help the Less Fortunate foundation. She finally felt that Kortville had enough local passion to make the food pantry and community closet come to fruition without outside help. And that meant she was free to cut her final ties to Trevor.

"Veronica, thank you so much for your dedication to the community needs center," Agatha said. "I now have faith that we're going to get it off the ground regardless of what Ron decides to do with his money. This is a lifelong dream of Wilbur's, and we never could have done it without the financial support from the Help the Less Fortunate foundation."

She nearly choked. "They contacted you?"

"Someone by the name of Mr. Cunningham the Fourth.

He said they'd give us everything we asked for. I don't even know what we asked for."

All the progress and contacts and possibilities Veronica had seen coming to light today slipped through her fingers. She'd made her decision to scrounge and improvise, instead of taking Trevor's money. Except he had gone ahead and held up his end of the deal. Everything would be taken care of. She looked at Matt heading to his pickup with Jenny. Everything except what she wanted.

She forced a smile for Agatha. "I'm glad I can do something that makes a difference."

"Honey, you've made a huge difference. We are so proud to have you call Kortville home." Agatha wrapped her arms around Veronica and hugged her hard.

Veronica's stomach clenched. This was her town, and she couldn't let it down. As Agatha walked away, she opened her phone and dialed. "Paige, where's that car you promised me?"

"You read my mind." She laughed. "We're in a limousine, entering the edge of town."

Her one hope that logistics would make the journey to Chicago impossible tonight was dashed. "We?" If she had to do this, she at least hoped to have the four-hour drive to mentally prepare herself.

"I talked Trevor into coming with me. Where are you right now?"

She gave Paige directions to the park and waited by her defunct car for the limousine to show up.

It pulled around the corner just as Matt got back out of his truck and walked toward her. "I can give you a ride to your trailer if you need."

"Thanks, but I've got one." She willed him to leave quickly. Seeing her jump into the back of a limo would reaffirm every spoiled thought he'd had about her since they'd met.

The limo pulled to a stop. The back door opened, and Trevor himself stepped out, wearing a starched suit and blinking in the sunlight. His eyes widened in horror as he focused on her. "Get in before anyone sees you looking like that."

Hello to you, too, Veronica thought. "What's wrong with how I look?"

"You look like a teenager who just rolled out of bed."

The T-shirt she'd pulled on over her dress had helped the townspeople see her as one of them and had made Matt look at her with the same gleam that Barney's dog had when he was eyeing the unattended plate of burgers earlier. "It's an unintimidating look. People here seemed to like it."

Trevor adjusted his earpiece, no doubt tuning in to a phone conversation only he could hear. He glanced back into the limo. "Paige, are you taking notes on the Myers offer?"

"Yes, sir," was the faint reply from inside. With both of them consumed by their earpiece conversation, Veronica would essentially be alone with her thoughts after all.

Trevor held the door and motioned for her to climb in. "I hope you have a change of clothes and some shoes for tonight. We're already running late."

"What are you doing?" Matt asked, his voice low.

She hazarded a glance at him. His jaw was clenched, and his gaze was lethal. It was sweet that he was so protective of her. "Trevor, this is Matt Shaw, my boss at Kortville Construction. Matt, this is Trevor Cunningham the Fourth."

Trevor held out his hand and added, "Veronica's fiancé."

• • •

Matt looked from the hand to the prick it was attached to and then to Veronica. She looked surprised as well as guilty.

Apparently, she thought she could play him and assume he'd never find out the truth.

And he had been played. She'd kept up the sham of construction work with such dedication that he'd believed she was doing it for the career she'd claimed she wanted to start. Then she'd shuddered and melted with such conviction in his arms that he'd believed her attraction to him was genuine, that the other guy had never touched her, that she was thinking of no one but Matt.

He squeezed the guy's soft, cold hand. It was immature, but he didn't care. In fact, he hoped he broke a few fingers. Matt felt like the clichéd all-brawn, no-brains lowlife who someone else's fiancé had been slumming with.

"I assume you'll have her back for work by seven a.m. sharp on Monday," Matt said, although he had no such delusions. No wonder she hadn't kissed him or promised to wear her sexy shirt to work on Monday.

"I hope not to have her back here at all," Trevor said, confirming his expectations as well as his fears.

"Stop it, you two. One way or another, I will return," Veronica said with a cheerful smile.

"I won't hold my breath." Matt reluctantly released the jerk's hand.

"I don't know why you'd want to," Trevor told her, tentatively flexing his fingers.

Veronica gave him a light push on the back, nudging him into the limousine. Then she looked back at Matt. "It's not what you think."

"Are you going to marry that puffed-up guy with the dorky thing sticking out of his ear?" *Please say no.*

"We'll talk about it when I come back." Veronica slid into the limousine and closed the door.

She didn't say no.

She wouldn't return. For the second time in three years, Matt watched a woman drive away from him back to her sophisticated city life. *Fool me twice...*

• • •

"I think he broke my knuckles," Trevor moaned.

Veronica's instinct was to defend Matt, but she had no plausible explanation for his behavior, other than he was extremely angry with her and took it out on the guy who had stepped in the middle before she'd had a chance to set Matt straight.

"Let me see." Paige inspected his hand and bent each finger. Then she dug a highball glass out of a cabinet and filled it with ice. "Hold this. It'll make your hand feel better."

"It'd feel better if you topped the ice with whiskey," Trevor said.

Paige rolled her eyes. "Don't be a baby. You'll be fine."

Veronica sat on the seat watching them, feeling like a fifth wheel. Of course. Why hadn't she seen this before? Trevor might be a typical clueless man, but it was obvious to her that Paige was more than a dedicated personal assistant. She was completely in love with her boss. What woman wanted to see the man she was in love with marry another woman?

"Before you get drunk, we need to talk about why you need this merger so badly," Veronica said. As tempting as it was to liquor him up and work out the points he would have objected to, she wasn't going to build the foundation of her life on deceit and trickery. It might be too late to convince Matt of her pure intentions, but she wasn't trying to fool or take advantage of anyone.

"Isn't it obvious?" Trevor said. "I make what your dad needs."

"So, you sell it to him and make a profit off those sales. You don't give up the potential sales you could have made to his competitors."

"The merger makes sense," Trevor argued. "His office building is on the verge of demolition, and I have the space."

"Yeah, you have a gorgeous office building. Those marble floors and fancy chandeliers don't come cheap, do they?" She thought of Matt's simple—some would argue shabby— office. It was functional and, like Matt, didn't pretend to be something it wasn't.

Matt's workmanship spoke for itself. His mere presence took her breath away.

"What's your point?" Trevor snapped.

"I think you need to restructure your lease agreement or break it entirely. Not merge with my father. Not marry me." Veronica held her breath. She was taking a big risk, and she'd gone about it backward. She hadn't insured he wouldn't take back the promised funding for the food pantry and community closet before she'd plunged in.

Trevor glared at Paige. "I thought you made a deal with her."

"Wait," Veronica said. "Hear me out first. I have something better to offer than marriage and a merger blessing. I can run some figures and analyze your lease situation to get your business back on track and your profitability up to par. If you think the analysis is worth more than a toss in the recycling bin, Help the Less Fortunate cuts the check for the Kortville community needs center as promised."

Trevor frowned.

"You have nothing to lose," Paige pointed out. "If her advice is crap, you don't have to pay anything, unless she changes her mind and agrees to marry you again."

Veronica knew her advice wasn't crap, but she still hadn't

gotten anyone to take her seriously and believe that what she had to say was worth anything. And that meant she hadn't secured a darn thing for the needy citizens of Kortville, might very well have destroyed Matt's trust in her for nothing, and could be strong-armed into marrying someone she barely tolerated.

Veronica stood just inside the doorway at the charity dinner, wishing she were peddling sushi with Pauline or in a booth at the diner with Matt and Jenny. No one had noticed her yet. Maybe she could still escape.

"Thank goodness you made it. Paige promised you would, but I was getting worried," Mother said, her panic contained to the brighter than usual hue of her blue eyes. "Come over to our table and distract your father. He's getting all worked up that Trevor isn't paying attention to the needs of his company, and if it's this bad now, how much worse is it going to be after the merger?"

"He has a point," Veronica murmured.

"Exactly. That's why he needs you to make sure that Trevor continues to have a reason to care."

Right. Veronica wished she was on top of a roof and could take her frustration out on pulling shingles, but like her mother, she kept her emotions bottled inside as she crossed the room. She started to sit in the reserved space and then stared, dumbfounded. Across the table, Ron was leaning his chair back on two legs as he laughed and joked with a society matron at the next table. "What's he doing here?"

"I invited him," Mother said. "I thought he should see what my life is like before he constantly judges it. So far, he's ignored your father, but he seems to be enjoying himself."

That was one word for it. If he leaned any farther back, his chair was going to tip over, and he'd find himself flat on his back. Even more disturbing, the normally prim and proper president of the women's social club, who pursed her lips in disapproval whenever Veronica used her dessert spoon to stir her coffee, laughed boisterously at Ron's jokes. She eyed Ron's precarious balance with such glee, Veronica was afraid she might purposely fall over on top of him.

Veronica looked away from the pairing that was sure to be the talk of the town for weeks and strolled around the table, kissing her father on the cheek. "Hello, Dad."

"Running off to join a construction company is the craziest stunt I've ever heard a kid pulling. Your mother and I have been so worried about you," he said gruffly.

"You didn't have any reason to be. I was taking care of myself." Even though she'd managed to put construction work in the same league as joining the circus. She took a deep breath. "I hear you're having some concerns about the merger."

"Nothing that nailing down a wedding date won't cure," Dad replied glibly.

"Actually, I disagree. Your business concerns are well founded, and you should take them to heart. I'm going to do some analysis for Trevor and show him how he can restructure his business to avoid the merger altogether and make his company more profitable and stronger on its own. I'd be happy to do the same for you."

"Don't you worry about that. I have my business under control."

She bit down on her exasperation. He didn't have it under control, and she didn't appreciate being patted on the head and told to go plan a wedding. She surveyed the room one more time, wishing she were back in the Laundromat brainstorming ways to help the community with Becca.

Trevor stood by a window, covering his earpiece with one hand while gulping a drink with the other. Paige was just outside the entrance, clearly wishing she were at his side. Veronica did a quick survey of their table. Other than Ron, Mother hadn't planned any extra place settings.

"Excuse me, Dad. I'm needed somewhere else right now." Veronica left the table and wove her way out the door to Paige. "I need a favor."

"What's that?" she asked, crossing her arms over her chest.

Veronica understood her wariness. She wouldn't want to go from being the personal assistant of the man she loved to working for him *and* his fiancée. "I need you to take my place at dinner, so I can go back to Trevor's office and crunch those numbers he needed."

"Why would you want to do that?"

For so many reasons; she hardly knew where to start. Her best bet to get Paige on her side was to lay all her cards on the table. "Because these dinners drive me crazy, and marrying someone I don't love just to make other people happy makes me even crazier. I can get both Dad's and Trevor's businesses to run better if they give up this merger plan. Please help me, Paige."

She smiled. "I'm in. And…will you be pissed if I make a move on the man you don't love and don't want to marry?"

"I will thank you from the bottom of my heart if you steal him away from me," Veronica promised. "If you can convince him to honor what Help the Less Fortunate has already offered to Kortville, I'll even take you wedding dress shopping."

Paige dangled a set of keys in front of her. "The gold one opens his office. Go crazy with your calculator and wish me luck."

• • •

Matt's foul mood continued through Monday morning. When he pulled his truck in front of the convenience store, his gaze naturally shifted across the street to Veronica's trailer. He hadn't seen or heard from her since she'd gotten in the limo Saturday afternoon. He didn't expect that he ever would. She might as well have shouted her choice from the rooftops for as clear as she'd made her intentions known.

Despite that, her trailer looked homey and inviting, as if she'd step out of it and walk toward him at any moment. Her small section of grass was trim, green, and weed-free. The planter of pink-and-white impatiens swung above the front window. Craft yard signs proclaiming WELCOME FRIENDS and HOME SWEET HOME camouflaged the concrete blocks.

The clock in his truck rolled to seven, and Matt took a final swig of coffee and got out of his truck.

"Hey, you can't work here in the mornings. Did you forget about Barney's doughnut business?" Veronica called cheerily as she crossed the street to him.

Matt froze, astonished she was there, let alone that she'd troubled herself with a trivial detail. And darn it, how dare she wear that Kortville baseball T-shirt with her jeans, picking up their flirting from the picnic as if she hadn't run off for the weekend with her rich, successful fiancé? What kind of game was she playing with him? "I'm finishing the outside siding. Grab a hammer."

"No thanks. I'm saving us both the misery of having me mess up another construction job."

"What'd you come back for if you're not working for me?" He tried to squash it, but hope swelled in his chest that maybe, just maybe, she'd come back because of him.

"Don't worry. I told you I'd come, and I did. And I'm working for you, too. I'm picking up a doughnut, and Barney's giving me a ride to the office." She flashed him another smile and started for the store entrance.

Matt reached out and caught her arm. "Why did you wear that today?" She'd tied up the extra bagginess at her waist, turning the shirt into a fashion statement that was uniquely hers.

"It was supposed to make you happy. Honestly, Matt, I think it's making you grumpy. Maybe we should try the kiss instead."

He released her arm. "I'm trying to run a business." And trying not to let her sweet-talk him into giving her a free ride. And trying not to get his heart broken. He hadn't done a single one of those successfully since she'd blown into his life.

She patted his shoulder. "I'm doing everything I can to make sure you run that business as smoothly as possible. Your finances are going to be in tip-top shape at the end of the month."

He didn't care about his finances. He'd rather spend the day—the week, the month—being with her, even if she messed up every job and made more work for him. "Where were you all weekend?"

"If I told you I was working, would you believe me?"

"No," he said flatly.

"All right, then. Have a great day, Matt."

That was it? She wasn't going to try to convince him? Wasn't going to prove that she'd thought of him and only him all weekend while she'd been with her fiancé? And why should she? Veronica hadn't lied to him before. She had no reason to attempt to soothe the jealous streak in his heart when he wouldn't believe her anyway.

But he still wasn't ready for her to walk away. "How'd you get Barney to give you a ride? Does he have a pile of rancid meat he's going to unload on you?"

Her guileless blue eyes sparkled. "Now that we've settled on a date for my trailer to be taken away and work on the baseball field is set to begin, he's offering me the fresh goods."

"What? When?" Had she come back to clear out her stuff before she returned to her old, better life? And who was taking out the trailer if he hadn't been told about it? Ron had hired him to clear out all the other trailers.

"Next week."

One more week to put up with her before she went back to her old life. In fact, he didn't even have to put up with her. He could simply ignore her while she passed the time in the office. Everyone won.

Veronica got back the lifestyle she was accustomed to.

The town got its promised funding from Ron's sale of the distribution center.

Matt got his work done in peace and preserved his quality reputation.

So, why did he feel like he was losing everything?

Matt avoided the office and Veronica's trailer for three straight days. In that time, he heard rumors about Ron charming society matrons and whacking his son-in-law in the shins with his cane. There were even whispers about Trevor Cunningham the Fourth calling Wilbur to personally assure him the funding for the community needs center was still on track and Agatha swearing that a woman named Paige had been in the background feeding him every word. There was not a single rumor about Veronica having a fiancé or even being present at the party where all these events had occurred.

On Wednesday afternoon a water emergency at Mrs. Parker's farmhouse sent him scrambling to do repairs, even though he'd already promised Glenda he could be off work early so she'd be free for one of her athletic manager commitments.

He needed to find a back-up sitter before Jenny got out of school. Heidi was working, and she'd been counting on him to take care of Stephanie. The grocery store was short-staffed, so Becca couldn't take the afternoon off. Pauline couldn't leave a diner full of customers. In desperation, he called Ron, who didn't answer his phone.

So, Matt swallowed his pride — and his resolve not to have any contact with Veronica — and called her. "What are you doing right now?"

"Your computer was low on memory so I added another gig. I also downloaded the latest update to your financial software."

Whatever he'd expected her to say, it certainly wasn't geek-speak. Naturally, coming from her mouth, she managed to make it sound sexy, too. "Where did you go to get that?"

"Online computer store, next-day shipping. You only like to *think* you're out of touch with civilization," she teased. "You're really just a mouse click away."

Matt grunted. "How much did that set me back?"

"Not as much as you think."

Right. He'd called for a reason. It took him a beat to remember what that reason was. "I have a huge favor to ask you."

"I'm all yours."

Talk about a fantasy image. Matt cleared his throat and focused on the chaos around him. "I'm at Mrs. Parker's — the farmhouse where we fixed the gate."

"*You* fixed the gate," she corrected. "I passed out and slept the rest of the day on your couch."

"Yeah." He didn't need the reminder of how sweet and peaceful she'd looked or how she'd snuggled under the blanket as he covered her or how shaken he'd been for the rest of the day knowing she'd made herself at home in his house. "I'm trying to fix a broken water pipe. Glenda would normally be on her way to school to pick up Jenny and Stephanie, but she had another commitment this afternoon, and Mrs. Parker is standing ankle-deep in water trying to salvage a bunch of pictures and stuff before they get wet."

"So, you want me to pick up the girls?"

Add "reading his mind" to the list of her attributes. A woman simply could not come packaged more perfectly. "Please. I'm trying to find someone else to watch them because they can't come here. The farmhouse is a lake, and there's no running water. But so far, I haven't had any luck finding anyone who's available."

"How about I take them to your house? We'll play dress-up and braid hair."

There it was, Matt's terrifying fear that Veronica's influence would turn his niece into a girl who expected weekly manicures and jetted off to the city for expensive shopping trips. "I don't like to encourage that kind of thing."

"You're morally opposed to braids?"

She made him sound like a fool. "No, of course not." The wrench slipped as he worked to unscrew the old pipe from the fitting. He needed to get off the phone, so he didn't have his head and arms tipped at odd angles. "It would be a godsend if you could watch the girls. Just don't let Jenny dress up like any of those pop stars in the magazines that Stephanie's always showing her."

"You got it."

He didn't trust Veronica not to run off with a rich city man. He didn't trust her not to ruin his town. But he had no choice but to trust her with the most valuable thing in his life—his niece. "Thanks, I owe you."

"I think I can come up with a good way for you to show your appreciation."

So could he. A little whipped cream. A lot of tongue. Matt clicked off the phone and slipped it into his tool belt. It stopped him from flirting back. It didn't stop the fantasy.

· · ·

After a quick confirmation call to Matt and another one to Stephanie's mom, Heidi, the teachers released the smiling girls into Veronica's care. She didn't take offense to the calls. No one was out to get her. They were following protocol to keep the children safe and accounted for.

She contemplated if she'd taken a step up or down by trading in her construction hardhat to become a daycare provider, as the three of them walked along the sidewalk to Matt's house. Jenny and Stephanie chattered about their day at school, their classmates, and their plans for the afternoon.

Veronica could see why Matt's world revolved around his niece. Knowing that he'd trusted Veronica—even if she was a last resort—with the most important person in his life was a step in the right direction. She needed his trust. She'd lost it the moment she'd entered the limousine with Trevor. So, she'd start over, and she'd show him she was on his side in every way that mattered.

They rounded a corner to the next block as Ron took a step up his driveway from the mailbox at the end of the street. "Hi, Mr. Walker," the girls chorused, skipping ahead to greet him.

Ron leaned on his cane and greeted them with a smile. His eyes narrowed as he looked beyond them to Veronica. "Where are you all going?"

"We're having a girls' afternoon," Jenny said.

His eyes widened. "You're babysitting? You could be in Chicago having a spa day with your mother."

Veronica smiled at the girls bouncing around at her side. "I'd rather be babysitting," she said honestly.

"Mr. Walker, can Stephanie and I see your new gazebo?" Jenny asked.

"There's not much to see yet, but you can look." Ron waved them toward the backyard and then rubbed his fist against his chest as he turned back to her. "I thought you were going to be at the dinner Saturday night, but you never showed up."

She resisted pointing out that she'd been there, however briefly. He'd just been too preoccupied to notice. "I had some things I needed to do in order to prove to certain people that marrying me is a bad idea."

He leaned heavily on his cane, his other hand still pressed to his chest. "When you sent me that e-mail about how you were going to leave your family, it wasn't supposed to play out like this. I didn't want Angela to go through the pain of losing you like I went through when she left home. I made you a horrible deal, so you'd see how awful life was here in comparison to what you had."

"Life in Kortville is not awful. I love it so much better than a high-society city life."

"Then when Angela came to pick you up, you'd be so grateful for the life she'd given you *and* I'd be reunited with my daughter again," Ron continued. "My half worked out, but Angela is heartsick that you don't want to come home, and she's worried about the future of her husband's business."

His twisted logic made her head hurt. "So what's your solution this time? Do you have a gravel truck ready to unload on me to humiliate me into returning home?"

His mouth twisted with regret. "I'm sorry about the cement and the gazebo. I was desperate, and everything got out of hand. If you're free tomorrow, I can take you to the distribution center and get you acquainted with the people you'll be working with."

She would have given up her last pair of shoes for him to extend this offer when she first knocked on his door, but since then she'd discovered taking what others handed out was much less rewarding than what she could create on her own. "Thank you, but your company is being well managed. The financials are in good shape. You have a lot of interested buyers, so you can get a fair price. You don't want me coming in and messing all that up."

"Then what should I do with it?" he asked as Jenny and Stephanie returned, running down the driveway, their schoolbags bouncing against their backs.

"Sell it and give the profit to the town's causes like you planned."

His gaze narrowed in on her. "Maybe if I sell it, the proceeds should go to you. You seem like you could use some help getting started—enough money to buy a place of your own, a little cushion until you have a steady paycheck."

She shook her head. "I'm working on the steady paycheck thing. I have some plans."

"Come on, Miss Veronica, let's go. I really, really want to try on lipstick," Jenny begged.

"And I want a braid that swirls around my head," Stephanie added.

Ron sighed. "Go have fun, but I expect to hear all about these plans of yours as soon as you have a free minute."

"'Bye, Mr. Walker," the girls called, immediately skipping down the sidewalk.

Yes, she had plans. For this afternoon, they were all about two little girls who had wormed their way into her heart. But for her own life, her options were not narrowed to only what her father and grandfather offered to her.

She'd started taking control of her life on Saturday in the back of the limousine. Now it was time for her parents to see her as a competent adult and a business equal. She pulled out her phone and dialed. "Mother, it's Veronica. I need to schedule a meeting with you and Dad, nine a.m. tomorrow. Just the two of you. You'll find out what it's about when you get here."

She slapped her phone closed and quickened her pace to catch up to Matt's niece.

. . .

Matt peeled off his work boots and left them by the door. The pipe job had required more extensive repairs than he'd anticipated. The farmhouse was falling apart, and Mrs. Parker couldn't afford to put more than a Band-Aid on the problem. Which meant he'd likely be called out there again soon, but not to gut it and transform it back to its former glory, like it deserved.

He'd stew over that later. Right now, he needed to focus what was left of his energy on his niece. The house smelled like it used to when he'd come down for a weekend visit with Steve and Leah. Food was cooking in the kitchen. He hadn't planned ahead to have something ready for when he got home.

He strode through the entry to the living room and paused. Jenny was cuddled against Veronica on the couch, just like she used to curl on Leah's lap. She was wearing her Easter dress and reading aloud. Her legs were tucked under her, but he could see her Sunday shoes peeking out under the dress. Her normally stick-straight hair was a mass of curls, which Veronica's fingers absently threaded their way through.

His chest hitched at the adorable, maternal sight. This was the life Steve and Leah had wanted for their daughter, the life he'd never quite been able to duplicate alone. If only he'd been dating Veronica when he returned from the city to take his brother's place. Unlike Kimberly, she would have toughed it out and given Jenny the comfort and attention she needed.

Jenny looked up and noticed him. She tossed the book aside and bounded across the room. She jumped on him, wrapping her arms around his neck and dangling her fancy shoes off the ground. "Uncle Matt, you're home."

"And you are all dressed up and looking gorgeous." He squeezed her tightly, aching with the knowledge of how much Steve would give for the chance to hold his daughter one more time. "What's the occasion?"

"We made you supper."

"Did you?" Matt let her babble about the ingredients for beef Stroganoff and how they'd sent a big bowl home with Stephanie and her mother. Then he shifted his gaze to Veronica. She was sitting perfectly still on the couch, smiling at him and Jenny.

Veronica wasn't Leah, and Matt wasn't Steve. He couldn't make her play house with him just so Jenny could grow up with the family fate had cruelly snatched from her.

"Sorry I kept you here so late," he said. "I can take over now."

Her smile didn't waver, but her eyes dimmed, making her expression almost bittersweet as she rose off the couch. "Of course. Good night, Jenny."

Jenny pulled away from his embrace and ran to Veronica. "But you were going to stay for dinner."

She reached for Jenny's hand and squeezed it. "Sorry, sweetie. That was up to your uncle, remember? You have a lot to tell him. You can do that without me around."

He *did* want her around. In fact, he wasn't sure that he ever wanted her to leave. But he didn't want her to be a stand-in for his sister-in-law any more than he wanted to go through the motions for his brother. Steve was gone, and everything Matt wanted in his future was in this room. The thought didn't just scare him. It terrified him.

"Of course you can stay for dinner," Matt backpedaled. "You went to the trouble of cooking, plus made enough to give to another family. You not only helped me out of a tight spot but ensured I get to relax for the rest of the evening."

"Yes!" Jenny danced around the living room.

Veronica's face lit up again in a brilliant smile that told him dinner wasn't the only thing she was hoping to stick around for. "In that case, let me wash my hands, and I'll start serving. I believe everything is ready."

Oh yes, his attraction was blazing hot and intensified every time he saw her. It didn't matter that he'd already learned the hard way he had nothing to offer a beautiful woman who already had it all. Somehow he had to get through the rest of the evening while remembering that he had pride and integrity—and a niece watching his every move.

"What needs to be done to finish dinner?" Matt asked, after he'd cleaned up and then sent Jenny to wash her hands. He suddenly felt awkward and out of place in his own kitchen.

Veronica turned off the Crock-Pot and ladled the

heavenly smelling food into a serving bowl. "You can set the table. We're having two courses."

Two courses, and she'd pulled out Leah's fancy Christmas serving dish when eating the meal straight from the Crock-Pot would have sufficed. Nope, she was not an imitation of his sister-in-law. He needed to catalog everything she did that didn't fit with his lifestyle to remind himself of why she would never be satisfied with his way of life.

Jenny skipped into the kitchen. "I'll set the table."

"You're wearing makeup." As if that wasn't enough to make Leah roll over in her grave, Jenny's hair sparkled with glitter.

"We had fun being girlie," Veronica replied, winking at Jenny. Her hair shimmered more than usual, too.

Matt couldn't fathom why anyone thought glitter in hair was a sensible thing to do. Steve and Leah certainly wouldn't have understood, either. He'd tried so hard to follow their example, but faced with glitter and makeup, he felt like he'd failed. "The only thing I asked of you was to refrain from being girlie."

"You said don't dress like a pop star," Veronica corrected. "So we skipped the meat dresses and the neon hair dye. We didn't go overboard."

This wasn't overboard? Well, he'd wanted a reality check, and Veronica had delivered. "Jenny's only eight years old. She's too young for that stuff."

Veronica glanced at him as she stirred the contents of the Crock-Pot. "She knows she can't wear it every day. There's an art to applying blush and eyeliner. It's never too early to start practicing to get it right."

"She let Stephanie and me put on our own makeup, and then we got to put it on Veronica's face, too," Jenny said, her excitement undimmed by Matt's grumpiness.

He narrowed his eyes at Veronica. Maybe the glitter was Jenny's handiwork, but there was no way a child had applied the makeup on her smooth, glowing face.

"And then we washed it off so you wouldn't have a heart attack thinking I was going to take her to stand on a street corner, and I applied it like it is now." Veronica took the serving dish to the table. "I didn't corrupt her. I didn't make her grow up and not need you while you were gone. She's still your little girl."

Matt took a deep breath. She'd voiced his fears, and they sounded ridiculous coming from her lips. Jenny was his little girl, and she would always be Steve and Leah's girl, a child they had loved wholeheartedly and would have loved regardless of how much makeup or glitter she paraded around in. Girliness wasn't a superficial flaw that needed to be wiped out. Jenny just needed someone to connect with who understood her love of pretty, feminine things. And in that respect, she was now also Veronica's girl.

While Veronica cleaned the kitchen after dinner, Matt coaxed Jenny into taking a bath. She protested, trying to save her curls. Veronica offered to braid her wet hair so it would be wavy in the morning, and Matt gave in. But if he was honest with himself, he had to admit that it was simply an excuse to keep her in his house longer.

After the braids were secure, Jenny tried to stay awake with the grownups but fell asleep on his lap as he read her a chapter of *Charlotte's Web*. Once he returned from carrying her back to her bedroom and tucking her in bed, his anticipation built. He had an entire evening ahead of him with a beautiful woman who cared about his niece and the life he'd built in this town.

Veronica was no longer sitting on the couch. Instead, she was covering the dining room table with stacks of papers.

"What are you doing?" Disappointment and confusion settled over him. They weren't going to get comfy on the couch and make out?

She turned and smiled. "I want you to be the first to know I'm not going to take over Ron's distribution company, and I'm not marrying Trevor. I'm starting my own financial consulting company, and I want to work for you in that capacity."

He opened his mouth but no words came out. He'd been gearing up to kiss her, and she was setting up a business relationship. Was that really all she thought of him? What about the flirting and the kisses they'd shared? Had he been nothing more than a crush, and she'd already lost interest?

"Have a seat." She tapped the empty chair next to her. "Let's start with cash flow. This is your current bank balance."

Or now that she knew to the dollar how much he was worth, was she no longer interested? Just when she'd managed to convince him she wasn't superficial, she threw this evidence at him. "The bank had no right to tell you what my balance is."

"They didn't," she said cheerfully. "You had six months of unopened bank statements on your desk, which I reconciled."

She didn't seem fixated on the lack of zeros and commas in the number, so maybe he was overreacting.

"You're running a business," Veronica continued. "Someone in the company should know how much cash you have to buy supplies. If you're not going to take the responsibility, then it falls to your office manager, who at the moment is me, but we'll get to that in a little bit."

The idea of her as his office manager held more than a little appeal. Only a few days ago, he hadn't wanted her touching any of his stuff, but now he liked the thought of having her fingers all over everything—especially him. He shifted in his seat and tried to concentrate on what she was saying.

"Here is the essence of your cash-flow problem. You're trying to collect from jobs you finished six months ago, while your suppliers are demanding you pay them in fifteen days." She'd researched a lot more than his bank balance to figure that out. Both his respect and his unease increased a notch.

"The economy's been in the tank. I've had to cut people some slack." He hadn't meant to let accounts receivable go unpaid that long. His intention was always to send out personal reminders and follow-up letters as Leah had done, but now that he thought about it, he wasn't sure he'd ever gotten that far down his priority list.

"I think that's the problem." Veronica covered his hand with her own and squeezed gently. "You've cut them so much slack they don't consider an invoice from Kortville Construction as something that *has* to be paid."

Okay, so he had quite a bit of outstanding work he hadn't collected on. But Steve never liked to make other people look bad. Matt especially didn't like how she was making *him* look bad. He wanted to flip his hand over and press his palm to hers, entwining their fingers together. Instead, he shifted his hand off the desk, breaking the contact. He might want her in his bed, but not out of sympathy.

"Look, you've never been broke before." Matt pushed back his chair so he could inhale a full breath without catching her exotic scent. "You don't get what it's like to live without an unlimited cash supply at your disposal. Everyone's going to make good. I won't refuse to fix their broken water mains and faulty electrical outlets until they've scraped together the cash."

She turned fully in her chair to face him. "Don't turn defensive on me, Matt; we're a team. I called your suppliers and was able to negotiate new terms where you now have thirty to forty-five days to pay and the payments will be electronically deducted."

"I can deal with my own business contacts." He jumped to his feet and started pacing the carpet. She made him sound incompetent at what Steve had entrusted to him. He had no chance of convincing her he had anything to offer when she was listing his faults down to the tiniest detail.

"I didn't set up a mega-business deal. I just negotiated some minor administrative details with the account managers, who usually are part-time employees with a community college education," Veronica explained. "The result gives you financial breathing room, and the electronic payments guarantee they get their money."

She'd done something so basic he'd never even thought to inquire about. Matt felt like he had nothing to offer Veronica that she didn't do better or couldn't get better somewhere else.

Veronica hated watching Matt grow more agitated by the minute. She needed to take him through the balance sheet, and she had some serious concerns that he was not getting his fair share out of the partnership with Ron.

"Talk to me before you make any more decisions or changes," Matt said, drumming his fingers on his thigh. As if having a longer grace period to pay the bills was a bad thing.

Veronica wanted to rub his neck until she'd smoothed out his rigid tendons. Instead, she picked up another file folder. "You need someone to do what I've done this week—keep up with accounts receivable, send reminder bills, make gentle phone calls, as well as keep your bank statements balanced so you don't get into overdraft trouble."

His eyes practically glazed as she talked. She tried to inject a little personal humor into her next item. "I'd also like to see a monthly plan to set aside some money to replace depreciating assets. Like, say, a wheelbarrow that's taken a lot of abuse lately."

He didn't crack a smile.

Apparently, they weren't at the point of sharing inside jokes. "Come here and look at these four scenarios I've worked up—hiring a part-time administrative assistant for twenty hours a week, hiring the same person for ten hours a week, hiring no one and doing everything yourself, and hiring an independent consultant to work with you."

Matt walked back to the table and glanced at the papers lying across it. His arm brushed her shoulder as he pointed to the column with the cheapest initial expense—doing nothing. If she turned her head, she could press her lips against the smooth bulge of his biceps.

"Looks like a no-brainer," he said.

Her brain was gone. She wanted to kiss him until neither of them could see straight. But she was staking her future on bringing Matt around—she couldn't afford to lose her focus. "Don't forget to factor in what your time is worth, the extra work you'll have to put in when you could be home with Jenny, the jobs you'll have to turn down."

He cut her off with a strong hand to her shoulder. "I'm not turning anything down. People will call in companies from other towns to do them, and then I'll be completely out of a job."

She covered his hand with her own and squeezed. "Then you need skilled labor to replace you on the job site or you need someone else in the office. I'd like to be that person."

"What?" He pulled his hand free and looked at her as if she'd taken a hard hit to the head. "You're already working for me."

She took a deep breath and stood to face him. She hadn't been nervous telling Ron, her parents, or Trevor what she wanted, but she was nervous now. As much as she tried to pretend Matt was the same as anyone else in town, he wasn't. He was more, so much more. "I'd like to do projections, crunch some numbers, and work up proposals for you. It could be very minimal. Say, five hours a week. That would be as a business consultant, so I'd expect a professional hourly fee."

His forehead crinkled in confusion. She resisted the urge to smooth it out. If she wanted him to see her as a professional, she couldn't allow her physical actions to betray her. And from the look on his face, she had a long way to go to achieve that goal.

"Then for the next, let's say, year I'd work another ten hours a week on your bookkeeping, business management, and administrative duties for a substantially lower fee." The work would guarantee a certain income, so she could eat and have running water while she got her core consulting business up and running.

"Let me get this straight." He cupped his hands around her elbows. "Instead of working for me for a month, now you want to work for me for a year, and you want a raise?"

Had her proposal sounded that greedy? She'd hoped it would be a win-win for both of them. "I'd be an independent contractor, so I wouldn't technically be your employee."

"What does Ron say about it?"

"This doesn't have anything to do with him. This is about you and your company." She'd given him her best proposal. She'd laid everything out for him, short of tattooing her feelings across her forehead. She didn't know whether to be grateful or cry that he was oblivious.

"I think it's a monumentally bad idea." Matt released her

arm and backed away.

She willed her voice not to choke up. She'd come too far to give up with her first rejection. She crossed the room to him and put her hand on his shoulder. "Would it be so hard to put a little faith in my abilities?"

"I'm not knocking your ability. It's your commitment I don't trust."

Still? Other than time, she had no way to prove she was here for the long haul. She wasn't sure she was patient enough to wait years for him to believe in her. Keeping one hand on his shoulder, she pressed her other palm gently against his bristled cheek and turned his head toward her. "I'm committed to Kortville—I explained that already. I'm dedicated to making you as successful as I can—as your employee, as a service provider with a vested interest, and as a fellow businessperson who wants to see you succeed for your own sake and for the sake of the town."

His cinnamon-brown eyes snapped to hers, heating her from the inside out. "A service provider?"

"Business service," she clarified. Although her needs suddenly felt a lot less businesslike and a lot more personal. She knew she risked her fledging professional reputation by focusing on the chemistry between them. But if she could convince him of how devoted her heart and soul were, he'd no longer see logistics and different lifestyles as obstacles. She could convince him he could count on her on every level.

She stood on her tiptoes and pressed her lips to his. She leaned into him, sliding her hands around his head and through the hair curling over the neckline of his T-shirt. She liked how he felt, overdue for a haircut, his body on edge.

She slid her fingertips over his temples and brushed lightly against his eyelids. He closed his eyes as she intended. She slowly massaged the bridge of his nose, feeling his tension drain away. She was doing this to him, relaxing him, drawing out the response she wanted him to feel. She could imagine doing this years from now after a hard day at work.

Her body tensed, and her hands froze. She couldn't start dreaming of forever while he was still dreaming up ways to push her out.

"Are you okay?" Matt's voice was warm and husky against her lips.

She tipped her head back and looked in his eyes. "More than okay when I'm with you." Then she moved her hands gently over his face again and pressed her lips to the hollow of his throat.

His pulse jackhammered beneath her lips. "I don't even know why you're here."

"I don't want to be anywhere else." For the first time, that was the absolute truth. She kissed her way up his neck and along his jawline, enjoying the feel of his facial hair against her cheek. She moved her hands higher up his head and brought his mouth down to hers.

His hot, sweet breath caressed her mouth, but Matt turned his head at the last second and her lips connected with his cheek instead. "Don't." His voice was raspy as he moved away from her. "I can't do this, not with Jenny asleep in the next room."

"Can't kiss me, or can't trust me to make your business better?" Right now the physical loss hurt most. Her arms ached to wrap around him again.

"Can't kiss you *and* can't make any business decisions… not when all I want is to kiss you and…more…all night long."

Chapter Ten

Veronica had taken care to present herself as the type of person her parents were accustomed to doing business with—dressed in a cream pantsuit, sensible heels, and pearls. Hopefully, they wouldn't notice that her hands had shaken as she'd applied her makeup.

The office door opened, and she walked down the hall to meet them. Instead, Matt stormed through the reception area straight toward her, holding a file folder of papers. His jaw was locked. His gaze was furious.

"What's wrong?" She didn't back up, refusing to let him intimidate her.

"Besides the fact that I didn't sleep at all last night because I couldn't stop thinking about kissing you?" His shoulder bumped against her as he pressed her back against the wall.

"Why does that make you so angry?" She raised her face and pressed her lips to his unshaven chin. Picking up where they left off would be perfectly agreeable to her if her parents weren't due to walk through the door at any moment.

"It wouldn't if you weren't trying to interfere with this." He waved the stack of papers, and she caught a glimpse of the partnership document. She settled her hand on his shoulder. "We didn't get around to talking about a few things last night, including the way you're dividing the profits within your partnership with Ron."

He pushed her hand away. "Our partnership is between him and me."

She cupped his face in both her hands, needing him to hear her out. "I'm not trying to get in the middle of it, but I want you to make sure you understand your rights. Because you're working full time in Kortville Construction and Ron's not, you're supposed to be taking a salary. Then you two can divide what's left equally. You've been dividing the profits without taking the salary into account."

"So that gives you the right to think you can dissolve our partnership?"

"Of course not. But I'm saying the three years of wages he owes you can be used for you to buy him out. It's exactly what you wanted!" She kissed his lips in her excitement, wanting to celebrate with him.

He jerked back. "This partnership ties Ron to Kortville. Don't cut him out, or you'll cut out the entire town." This time, his lips slammed on hers. There was no sweetness, no lingering, no gentleness.

She pressed her hands against the wall behind her. She wanted to caress him, to show him that she was part of his team. But he wasn't flirting with her, wasn't trying to build something with her. Yet she had too much pent-up desire they'd never acted on last night, and she wanted him, even if she knew he was touching her for all the wrong reasons.

His hand pushed away the lapel of her blazer and molded itself against her breast. Veronica moaned her acceptance of his touch. If this was how he destroyed his enemies, what a way to go down.

"What the hell is going on here?" her father thundered.

Matt dropped his hands, as if her skin was molten steel, and stepped back. "Excuse me. This…was completely inappropriate," he said, addressing her parents.

Then he looked at Veronica, his face a mask, with none of the desire he'd shown a moment ago. "The partnership stays in place. In the future, please refrain from giving any input into the way I conduct my business." He marched out of the office.

"Good lord, that man has turned you into trailer trash." Dad shuddered.

Veronica looked down at her disheveled blazer, hardly able to recognize the heat that had caused her rumpled state when Matt had turned his emotions to freezing. Regardless, she wasn't the type of person her parents would do business with if she looked and acted like they'd just witnessed. She wasn't their debutante daughter, and she wasn't a strong small-town woman, either.

Dad was right. She'd crossed the line into trailer trash.

She ducked into the hall out of sight and tucked in her shirt. Then she rubbed her fingers over what was no doubt her hopelessly smeared lipstick and hugged her cream blazer across her chest.

She took a deep breath and stepped back into the reception area. "Mother, Dad, welcome. I have everything set up in the conference room, so why don't you come on back."

"What the heck is going on?" Dad demanded. "Do you want to press charges against that overmuscled brawn who was mauling you?"

"Matt wouldn't never intentionally hurt anyone," Veronica said, horrified that he would think so. "Any passion between us is mutual." Actually, more on her side than his, but Dad didn't need the specifics.

"Is what I just witnessed what you've been doing the whole time we thought you were working construction?" Dad asked as she walked through the conference room doorway.

Veronica closed the door behind her. She had everything set up, exactly how she'd planned for their meeting. But she was back to proving that she was in Kortville for business and not in need of a family intervention. "His name is Matt, and the answer is an unequivocal no. I'm sorry you had to witness such poor judgment on my part. I won't embarrass you again."

"I'm not worried about you embarrassing me. I'm worried about you being taken advantage of and getting hurt. It's not too late to come back to your life in Chicago," Dad said.

"I didn't have a life in Chicago," she stated calmly. "All I had was an extension of your and Mother's lives. I had to come down here to make a life of my own."

"I'm almost afraid to ask. Are you making a life for yourself as a hooker or a construction worker?"

"George!" Mother said, sounding horrified. "You know your daughter better than that."

Sadly, Veronica wasn't sure that he did. "I'm not going to be a construction worker. I'm not going to work for Ron's distribution company, either." Her hands trembled. Telling them she wouldn't do what they'd never wanted her to do was easy. But explaining in no uncertain terms that she wouldn't follow the path they'd laid out for her and going so far as to open her intended path to their scrutiny and criticism was much harder.

"Well, for goodness sake, come home and marry Trevor," Dad boomed, standing in front of the table. "He's dying for you to come back."

"No, he's not. If that's what he told you, it's because he's too much of a wimp to admit that he's having second thoughts about the merger. Please sit down, Dad." She positioned herself at the head of the table. Mother followed her lead and sat next to Dad's chair.

"Of course, he's bound to have second thoughts if he sees you going at it with some other guy," he grumbled, finally taking his seat.

This was not the business meeting she wanted to have. But then Dad had never taken her ambitions seriously, even when her reputation had been pristine. "Regardless of my personal behavior this morning, you and Trevor don't need to merge. Your company will be stronger if you have a customer relationship with him and keep the businesses separate."

"You don't know anything about my business," he said belligerently.

He really didn't know anything about her, did he? She'd left home because she'd believed that was never going to change. But she wanted him to know what his daughter was really made of and how much of him she carried inside her. She held her hand out to him across the table and tried one more time. "Dad, all the business models and thesis papers I did for my MBA were of your business. I know your company inside out."

He grunted.

She ignored his rudeness. "I can tell you a dozen things off the top of my head to improve it, but you don't want to hear what I have to say, because you think my job is to smile and look pretty. If that's all you want out of me, I'll smile and look pretty when I visit you, but the rest of the time I'm going to use my brain and business skills on a company that will accept them."

"If you're not going to work at the job your grandfather promised you, what company are you going to use them on?" Mother asked. She, at least, had heard something Veronica was saying.

"I'm going to start my own consulting business."

"Your own business?" Dad thundered in disbelief, ruddiness rising in his cheeks. "Who's going to pay you for advice when you haven't worked a day in your life?"

"The lady who owns the diner. The people who own the Laundromat. The guy who runs the convenience store." She ticked them off confidently.

Mother gave a small smile as she stood and went to the coffee maker.

"You can't make a living off clients like that." Dad dismissed them all with a sharp gesture of his hand, nearly knocking over the mug that Mother handed to him.

Veronica didn't expect to make an income that her father would consider a comfortable living, but she was determined to make enough for herself. "I have to start somewhere."

Dad peered into the steaming cup. "You're not going to come back and marry Trevor?"

She shook her head. "I'm not. Paige knows it, even if he hasn't figured it out."

"Humph." He glared at his coffee without drinking it. For the first time he seemed to consider that she meant what she was telling him.

"It's no secret he wanted to merge because he got suckered into a long-term lease in that gorgeous new office building with too much space and too high of rent."

"The deal makes perfect sense," Dad argued. "Our building is so old it'd be cheaper to tear it down than repair it, and Trevor's building is in a better location."

"Have you looked anywhere besides his overpriced Taj Mahal? Industrial land is going for bargain prices right now. I worked up an estimate on a new building from a construction company that does quality work. Assuming you don't soup it up with marble floors and crystal chandeliers, you'll save more money going this route on your own than if you'd tried to merge the two companies." She slid a file folder across the table. "See for yourself."

Dad gave her a long look. She met his gaze without flinching, even though her heart was pounding painfully. She'd put everything she had into this proposal. She needed him to at least give it a chance. Slowly, he opened the file and glanced down.

"Kortville Construction?" He slammed the folder shut. "Are you crazy? I'm not hiring some Podunk company that's half owned by my father-in-law who hates me."

"Dad." She reached out and covered his hands with her own over the papers. "You're letting your emotions make your decisions, and that's not how you run a business. Use your head. Look at the numbers. You don't have to go with Kortville Construction, of course. Other companies can build what you need for roughly the same cost. But at least look at the proposal." She slid his hand away and opened the folder again.

Instead of slamming it shut, he studied it quietly for a minute. Then he looked up and met her gaze. "Where did you get such accurate financial numbers for my business?"

He really hadn't listened to a word she'd said. She bit back a sigh. "You've had them lying out on your desk at home for years. All I had to do was turn on your computer to learn more details. Like everyone else, you assumed that putting numbers together was beyond the capabilities of a pretty little blonde like me."

"I never thought you were stupid, Veronica."

"Well, you certainly never thought I had anything to say worth listening to." She stood up. She'd pushed; now she was ready to step back and let him make the next move—or not. "Take that home and look it over. Show it to your board and your vice presidents. Give me a call if you're interested or if you have any questions."

Dad stayed seated. He flipped through the file folder and drained his coffee. Finally, he looked up again. "I'll think about it."

Those four words might not have held any promise, but to Veronica they held a world of hope. For the first time, her father was seriously considering what she had to offer.

• • •

Matt's life had become a giant eggshell walk. His hormones were on edge, piqued and frustrated by half-finished encounters with Veronica. Worse, he was afraid she might have approached Ron with her plan for dissolving the partnership.

Ron had reconciled with his daughter. He'd also decided to go through with the sale of the distribution center, since Veronica no longer planned to run it. And rumors were thick that he intended to spend more time partying with his new city friends. Kortville Construction was suddenly his only remaining tie to the town.

Kortville needed that bond for Ron to go through with the funds he'd promised to various causes, instead of packing up and walking out on them for his new and improved life. Matt felt personally responsible for making sure he did whatever it took to keep Ron involved, even at the expense of giving up his right to run his company entirely on his own.

On Friday evening, he walked into the diner with Jenny, looking forward to a good meal that he didn't have to cook. After dinner, Jenny was sleeping over at Stephanie's house, and Matt had a quiet night to himself, which he intended to use to figure out a plan to keep his company running smoothly *and* to save his town.

He stopped cold as he spotted Veronica sitting in a booth

along the back wall. Her blond hair shimmered around her. Her pink button-down blouse stretched across her chest as she leaned forward intently.

This time, Pauline wasn't forcing espressos down her throat. The other customers weren't whispering about her or glaring over rumors about the destruction she could cause. In fact, Wilbur and Agatha, both wearing shirts in fluorescent plaid designs that made his eyes hurt, were sitting across from her and appeared to be hanging on to her every word.

"Aren't we going to sit down?" Jenny asked, confused. "Hey, Veronica's here. Let's sit by her."

"No, wait."

Jenny didn't stop, but Veronica froze at the sound of his voice. He watched her shoulders stiffen, but then she turned slowly and aimed her trademark wide smile at Jenny.

"Hi. Uncle Matt didn't tell me you were going to be here, too. Can we sit with you?"

"Jenny, she's already eating with someone else. We're not going to interrupt. Let's sit in this empty booth." Matt pointed to the one behind Veronica.

Veronica's smile didn't waver as she continued to focus on Jenny. "You can lean over the back of the seat. It'll be almost like you're sitting with me."

Except she didn't have to include Matt. He couldn't blame her. He'd made a point not to include her in anything since he'd last kissed her.

"Hello, Matt," Agatha said, her tone cool.

"You're interrupting our business dinner." Wilbur scowled at him. Matt didn't know what he'd done to upset the mayor, unless Veronica had been complaining about him.

"Business about what?" Jenny asked, standing on the bench directly behind Veronica and watching them. Matt was more than a little curious himself.

"About making Kortville a better place to live." Wilbur winked at her. Matt could interpret his words to mean just about anything, which told him nothing.

Veronica tipped her head to make eye contact with Jenny. "What did your uncle say about the clothes? Is it okay?"

"I guess so. He took the bags and didn't say anything." She shrugged.

"What was she supposed to tell me?" Matt asked Veronica. He hadn't wanted to run into her. But now that he had, he hated that she was ignoring him.

Veronica looked him straight in the eye. "Jenny and I went through some of her clothes when I visited last week." She held up her hand to stop any comment, although he didn't have anything to say. The fact that she could look straight at him and speak a full sentence put her light-years ahead of him in coherency.

"She's outgrown a lot of things in the past couple years. I asked her if she'd be willing to donate her old clothes to the community needs center Wilbur, Agatha, and I are starting, which she very generously agreed to." Eyes sparkling, Veronica reached behind her over the top of the booth and patted Jenny's arm. "This is going to be an effort of the entire town to provide free clothing to residents who can't afford to purchase the items for themselves or their kids. Thank you, Jenny, for doing your part."

Well, it wasn't exactly an effort of the whole town. It was a gift to the town from Ron.

"Times are tough, and decent people are struggling to make ends meet," Wilbur said. "Veronica convinced me I can increase profits in the Laundromat and get more votes in the next election if we set this thing up in the back room there."

"That's not why you're doing it," Agatha admonished.

"Yeah, I'm not going to increase my profits. I'm going to

kill them when I replace all those dryers," Wilbur grumbled.

"Think how many more people will pay to use machines that actually work," Veronica pointed out. This time she winked at Matt, and the blazing connection that he tried to pretend didn't exist flared to life.

"Did Ron give you the money for the project already?" He felt better knowing Ron was honoring his promises, but he still was surprised. Sales of entire businesses didn't go through quickly enough to produce instant cash.

"We're not waiting on Ron," Wilbur said. "And we decided we didn't want to be hemmed in by the rules of how we can and can't run the charity if we accept money from the Help the Less Fortunate organization. We are a self-reliant, do-it-ourselves kind of town."

"You should get connected with the Internet, Matt," Agatha added, "and Google Veronica in your spare time. She's dreamed up some amazing and innovative events to raise money and awareness for various charities in Chicago. We might be a low-budget town, but we're not going to sit around waiting for Ron or anyone else to go through with giving his money to a project. Veronica's jumping in and making it happen on her own."

"Not on my own." She looked embarrassed. "I've had a lot of help."

Matt slid into the booth with Jenny as Veronica bantered back and forth with Agatha and Wilbur. She'd seen a need in town, and she'd decided to fill it. He felt indebted to the town for everything they'd done for him after Steve and Leah died. But Veronica felt compelled to step up for the citizens when no one had gone out of their way to help her.

Matt's entire life still revolved around his brother and living out Steve's legacy, but he was starting to realize that maybe he was the only one who viewed his life that way. To everyone else, Kortville Construction was his company and Jenny was his charge. Maybe he needed to start thinking that way, too.

Except it would mean letting his brother go, and he wasn't sure he'd ever be ready to do that.

Jenny, who had moved on long ago and accepted him unconditionally as the parent in her life, spent a good part of the meal standing on the bench and popping her head over Veronica's booth, interrupting her conversation. Pauline delivered his food with the usual service, and then stopped to chat with Veronica and the Hollisters. Within seconds, she was sitting on the bench next to Veronica, ignoring a customer who was rating a row of espressos.

Heidi and Stephanie dropped in to pick up Jenny for her sleepover. Matt finished his dinner alone. Normally, he was comfortable with his own company, but tonight he wished Steve was across the table from him, offering his opinion on everything from the partnership to if he was a fool to want a relationship with Veronica to how he was doing raising Jenny.

Pauline never got around to giving him the bill so he left his money on the table and walked outside. He stood in the parking lot next to Veronica's ancient car with a brand-new taillight. Eventually, she came out and said her final good-byes to the Hollisters as they drove away.

"You got your car fixed."

She turned around, looking surprised to see him. "For now. Fred tells me it'll probably last for another three to six months, but it could stop running at any moment. Before I can afford to trade it in, it may turn out to be the most expensive car I've owned."

He shifted his feet. "So, um, we didn't part under the best circumstances last time."

She winced. "Sorry about my parents walking in on us."

"*I'm* sorry. I expressed my frustration in an inappropriate manner."

She lifted an eyebrow. "Frustration's what you were expressing? Really? Then maybe we should talk about the ramifications of ending the partnership, because I have a feeling it's not as dire as you imagine."

"It sounds like you have the community needs center covered," Matt admitted, because it was easier to talk about business than about what he'd hoped to accomplish with his hands up her shirt and his mouth covering hers. "But Ron had offered a lot more. He was going to donate lights on the baseball field and plumbing for the library."

"I haven't heard him back away from any of those things, have you? Whether he's your partner or not, he can still choose to donate."

She made it sound simple, while he felt like one wrong move would send everything spiraling out of control. "But I'd be taking away his connection to Kortville at a time when he already has one foot out the door, hanging out at high-society parties in the city."

She put her hand on his shoulder. "Sounds to me like you're going to have to trust him to go through on his word. Or better yet, trust the town to be resourceful enough to come up with another option if their first plan falls through. Still better, trust *yourself* that you can run a company without a partner to help you with the tough decisions, and you can do it just as well—or better—than your brother did."

He could take her first two suggestions but not the third. He'd never done anything better than Steve, and he certainly didn't want to now. And he absolutely could not trust himself with Veronica. She deserved so much better than a man feeling her up in his office, so much more than Matt, with his brother's small-town construction company, could give her.

Chapter Eleven

"I've seen the financials from the past. Leah kept good records. And I know what the financial picture is now. I'm not knocking your brother, but you have good business instincts, Matt," Veronica said. She was proud of what he'd accomplished in the three years since he'd plunged in and taken over. She wasn't sure that he realized how much he'd done or had anyone else point it out to him.

His phone rang before he could comment. He answered and listened for a moment. "Oh no, Mrs. Parker, not again. I thought we fixed that problem." He ran a hand through his hair as he kept listening. "If I didn't fix it right last time, then I'm not going to charge you again. Don't you worry about the cost. I'll be right there."

He sighed as he clicked off his phone. "So much for my business instincts. I'm losing money right and left on this job."

"Problems at Mrs. Parker's farmhouse again?" Veronica guessed.

"More pipe issues. The basement is filling with water, and she can't find the shut-off valve."

Veronica had hoped to convince him they should talk in

more detail about the partnership, so then she could show him the one file folder that she hadn't left on his dining room table, the one she'd never pulled from her bag the other night, the one that could match his hidden ambition that was directly opposite of his brother's. But nothing gave her a bigger thrill than seeing Matt in his element on a job site. "What are we waiting for? Let's go."

"No offense, but you're more of a distraction than a help when I'm trying to get things done."

She couldn't take offense when it was the truth. "I won't interfere. I admit I skipped the plumbing chapter in my book, but you might need an assistant to hand you tools. I know most of their names by now, so I should be able to get it right on the first try."

"An assistant would be handy. One I don't have the urge to take into my arms and strip her clothes off would be handier."

Oh my. Now there was an image guaranteed to get her libido revved up. "You can't be too choosy when these emergencies pop up. I'll try to make sure my clothes stay on, stay dry, and stay away from any wet concrete."

"You're hired." Matt held out his hand to her.

Instead of shaking it, she held it palm to palm. She walked with him to his truck, letting her thumb graze the hairs on the back of his hand. They rode in companionable silence, but Veronica's acute awareness of the man refused to allow her to relax completely.

The truck's headlights caught the sagging porch as Matt turned into the driveway. She caught her breath again. "Even in the dark, this place is majestic. I would sit on the porch and watch the sunset every day if I lived here."

"You'd fall straight through the rotten floorboards on the first night," Matt reminded her as he killed the engine.

"Once my favorite construction worker fixed them, I'd sit there," she amended. The thought of watching him work made her smile.

He slanted her a look across the dark cab. "I'm your favorite construction worker?"

If he had to ask, he had to be fishing for compliments. So, she shrugged casually. "Well, I really like Toby, too, but considering how young he is, I'll give you the edge."

"I think I can give you a more convincing reason to pick me." His lips brushed the tip of her ear.

She shivered and leaned closer so he could reach more than her ear.

"I hate this house," an elderly lady screamed as she toddled across the porch and down the rickety steps. "If I can't sell it, I'm going to trade it to you, Matt Shaw, for your overdue library book. There's a waiting list to check out *Charlotte's Web*, I'll have you know."

Veronica jerked apart before Mrs. Parker could see through the windshield. "You still haven't returned that book?"

Matt sighed and shifted to his side of the cab. "I meant to. I brought it out of the house and into the truck. I think it's under your seat." He sighed heavily as the librarian's muffled rant continued outside. "You know what I hate most about my job?"

"Useless assistants?" she guessed.

"No. Talking the customer off the ledge, instead of getting straight to work."

Really? Of all the nasty jobs he had to do, the part he despised was the one thing she was actually competent at? Veronica squeezed his hand. "You're in luck. Your assistant's not nearly as useless as we both thought. I'll take care of Mrs. Parker. You go do what you're best at."

She leaned over and touched her lips lightly to his cheek. Then she fumbled under the seat until she found the book. As she let herself out of the truck, she called, "Mrs. Parker, I have a present for you that's going to make you forget all about the problems with your house."

. . .

The truck headlights illuminated Veronica's trim, energetic silhouette as she jogged to Mrs. Parker. She put her arm around the lady and presented her the book with an exaggerated flourish. Whatever she said not only made the librarian crack a smile, but the crabby old lady actually laughed.

Matt would have needed at least a half hour to calm down Mrs. Parker to the point where he could make it in the house, and he certainly wouldn't have gotten her to smile. Veronica was by far the most efficient and effective assistant he'd ever had. Assistant, hell. Someone with this much talent deserved at least partner status.

As he collected his tools and headed into the house, Veronica still had her arm around Mrs. Parker. "Have you considered proposing to Matt that the two of you trade houses?"

He nearly stumbled. Trade houses? He'd never considered the concept. As much as he loved the farmhouse, he had to raise Jenny in Steve and Leah's house.

"Not straight up, of course," Veronica continued, still focused on Mrs. Parker. "Your gem here has to be worth more, but his house is in the middle of town and everything works just the way it's supposed to."

And Steve had once told him the house was only their starter, until they could afford something bigger for the large family he and Leah had planned to have.

"You make it sound so simple," Mrs. Parker said wistfully, echoing Matt's thoughts.

"It probably wouldn't be," Veronica admitted. "You'd have to get bankers and lawyers and surveyors and who knows who else involved. But I imagine the hassle would still be worth it for your peace of mind. Just think, you wouldn't have any stairs in your house and you'd only be a block from the library."

Matt trundled down to the basement, his head spinning. She'd shared her front porch fantasy and then turned around and practically handed the house to him, instead of trying to find a way to keep it for herself. If he read too much into it, he would start to believe all sorts of fanciful things that he hadn't entertained since Kimberly had killed his faith in happily ever after.

Eventually, Veronica joined him in the basement. "Mrs. Parker's going to bed. I promised her you had everything under control. I also promised you wouldn't catch a glimpse of her in her nightgown."

He certainly hoped Veronica could keep *that* promise. "I believe you're the one who wrestled everything under control. Hand me the big wrench, please."

She stepped around a puddle and picked up the tool, bringing it to him. "What else do you need?"

"Nothing right now. In a couple minutes, I'll want you to turn the faucet handles so we can test the connection and see if I fixed the leak."

Veronica didn't sit idly as she waited. She found a mop and began cleaning the floor until it was dry and quite possibly cleaner than Mrs. Parker had ever seen it.

It was the middle of the night by the time he was convinced he'd finally solved the problem and Mrs. Parker wouldn't have any more trouble with the water pipes. Veronica covered his hand with hers and snuggled against his side as he drove back to the diner to return her to her car.

"This is going to sound crazy, but I think tonight just became my gold standard of a date," Veronica said, not lifting her head from his shoulder.

It did sound crazy, but he wished he'd driven slower to make the ride last longer. "That had to have been the least sexy date on record."

She laughed.

He tried to laugh, too, as he shifted the truck into park, but his chest was too tight to allow one to escape. He still couldn't quite believe he was lucky enough to find someone like Veronica. There had to be a catch, something that he'd overlooked.

"I have a couple ideas to up the sexiness rating." She straightened in her seat and slid her fingers along his jawline. "Follow me back to my trailer."

"Of course I'll follow you, but just to make sure you get in the door safely. We've had a long night, and we're exhausted."

"We'll see how much energy reserves you have left when we get there." She pressed her lips to his and then slid out of the truck.

His heart thundered for the entire drive through town. If he had an ounce of self-preservation, he'd stay on the shoulder of the road and gun the engine as soon as she stepped over the threshold. Instead, he pulled into the trailer park directly behind her.

She walked to his truck and opened the door. "Come inside with me."

His instinct was to grab her hand and run to the bedroom before she changed her mind. Instead, he sat with his hands clenched on the steering wheel, summoning the last of his control. "Are you sure?"

"Yes." She held out her hand to him.

He'd wanted to make love to her in that ridiculously large bed since the moment he first showed her around the trailer. He wasn't fool enough to pass up the chance. He cut the engine of his truck and stepped toward her.

Instead of taking the hand she offered, he lifted her in his arms. For a moment she tensed, but then she relaxed and burrowed her lips against his throat. He tried to keep his gait steady as he walked inside her home, but he didn't feel as strong and all powerful as the last time he'd carried her in his arms. He felt vulnerable, like she could knock him over with a kiss.

He set her on the bed and leaned over to trail his lips down the column of her neck.

"You're seducing me," she murmured. Her body rose to meet his touch.

"Do you have a problem with it?" He wanted so badly to fill her every need, enough to ignore his body begging to be inside her now.

"No. But I want to return the favor."

"Later."

He concentrated on the tiny buttons of her shirt, drawing out each one, revealing an inch of skin and cleavage at a time. Then he slowly kissed his way down her chest to her navel, reveling in her staccato breathing.

Her fingers fisted at the hem of his T-shirt. She drew the shirt up, then abandoned it to smooth her hands around his waist. Her deepening arousal reflected in her eyes, in the heat of her hands as they sifted through the hairs at his belly. Knowing there was an answering infatuation on her side released the last of his misgivings.

He tossed aside his shirt, and then peeled back the fabric on her blouse. Lord, she was perfect—too perfect to settle for him on a permanent basis. But for tonight, she was all his, and he was going to make the precious moments they did have as perfect for her as possible.

Matt awoke alone to blinding brightness. He blinked and turned away from the light. He'd never paid attention to window treatments before, but at the first opportunity he was going to present Veronica with a set of very dark shades.

Outside, the rumbling of the ancient Oldsmobile grew louder, then silenced, followed by the opening of the trailer door. Wherever Veronica had gone, she was back. The energy in the trailer changed. The sun shining through the window was nothing compared to how she brightened a room.

Matt pulled on his jeans, stopping in the bathroom to brush his teeth and splash water on his face. When he got to the kitchen, she had two containers of yogurt and a box of doughnuts from the convenience store on the tiny table. Next to the food was a folder and a pen.

He ignored it all and went straight for her, clasping her in his arms and clamping his mouth over hers. He could smell her shampoo and feel the expensive silk of her blouse. In contrast, he was shirtless and smelled like yesterday's sweat. For the first time, it didn't make him feel inferior—not now, because of what they'd shared together. "Next time, wake me when you get up. I promise I'll make it worth your while."

She smiled and her cheeks flushed, but she pulled back from his embrace. "I thought maybe we could have a working breakfast before you pick up Jenny, since we never got around to what I wanted to talk to you about last night."

The last thing he wanted to do in his few remaining hours of alone time with her was pour over boring paperwork.

But he couldn't refuse her anything. At the farmhouse, they had been partners, working together the way he'd always envisioned his life with a mate would be. In the bedroom, they'd taken their partnership to another level and given him an entirely new appreciation for the word *harmony*.

She opened the folder and spread the papers across the table. "I worked up some cash flow estimates for the next couple years. They take into account the different office personnel scenarios, as well as buying new equipment."

He ate his jelly doughnut and reluctantly skimmed the figures while she opened a yogurt. "You're probably right that I'll need a new wheelbarrow, but not even ten of them would cost this much."

It pleased him that she'd keyed in her numbers wrong. They could put off the discussion until she fixed it. The yogurt looked much more appetizing on the spoon going to her lips. Maybe they could take the containers back to the bed and spend the morning promoting healthy eating. He sucked the jelly from his fingers. Or enjoying sweet confections.

She ignored his comment and picked up a pen, circling the variable items that altered the figures. Matt took another bite of doughnut. He couldn't make any sense of it. Considering he was consumed with creative ways to eat yogurt and jelly doughnuts, whatever came out of her mouth sounded like genius. His body was in no shape to analyze business figures.

"Those are all based on the assumption you don't build the new office for my father's company." She scooped up that stack and spread out another set of papers. "These are the estimates if the project is a go."

Matt stopped breathing, his entire body instantly chilled. "What are you talking about?"

"My father's company is looking to build a brand-new main office and production floor. It's at least twelve million dollars of construction work. I've recommended Kortville Construction to him."

The scorn on the faces of Mr. and Mrs. Jamison when they'd walked into his office and caught him feeling up their daughter remained vivid images. He didn't want to be their hired help, so they'd have one more excuse to look down their noses at him. "I don't do that kind of work."

"But you can, right? You have the skills. You just need more manpower and equipment. I sent him a preliminary proposal."

Matt shoved back from the table so abruptly his chair tipped backward as he stood. He ignored it, afraid if he picked it up he would smash it against the wall. "What possessed you to tie me up in a multiyear project without consulting me?"

She smiled and placed her hand on his bare chest. "You want to make this company profitable and successful—it's your dream. I talked to other contractors before I submitted the plan. I know it's a huge job that'll take a lot of time and new employees, but you have enormous profit potential."

Her hand scalded him. "Fulfilling my dreams is my problem, not yours. I don't want this job. Kortville Construction is a small-town, small-time operation, just the way my brother wanted it to be." His hands shook. For the first time, he knew his dreams were at odds with Steve's.

Her smile faded, and she pulled her hand back. "Why not? This is your chance."

"To be rich? To move in the same circles as you? Wake up, Veronica. That's not who I am. You can set me up to rebuild the Chicago skyline, but you're not going to turn me into that type of man."

As torn as he was about straying from his brother's vision, he'd thought Veronica had come to accept him for who he was. She'd certainly given every appearance of it last night.

But the indisputable proof that the man he was right now wasn't good enough for her stabbed the fatal dagger through his heart.

. . .

Veronica was still struggling to understand exactly what she'd done that was so awful. "I'm trying to improve your bottom line and the long-term success of the company. Changing the type of man you are has nothing to do with it."

"Doesn't it? You had your fun slumming with me. Not you can go home and live off that memory while you enjoy the pampered life that I'll never be able to give you."

She'd been so sure their lifestyle differences didn't matter anymore. After all, she'd adjusted to small-town life, and she loved it. "I'm not going anywhere. I plan to help you keep the bills and the payroll and the accounts receivable on the up-and-up through the whole job—and longer if you'll say yes."

Say yes. She willed him to say it.

The job didn't matter. Not compared to what she really wanted. It should have been obvious when she'd dedicated herself to straightening out his finances and discovering new profit potential. She had to have been completely dense not to have realized it last night as she worked side by side with him in the dingy basement and leaned against him in the dark truck. But she'd been oblivious, even when she'd given him her body.

She'd fallen in love with him. She'd fallen head over heels for Matt Shaw, his pure work ethic, his dedication to the town, and his adorable niece. She'd fallen for not just the man but the entire package.

Matt stared at her, his gaze eerily similar to the way he'd looked at her when she'd first arrived in town and he believed she was a threat to everything he stood for. "You went behind my back and arranged a deal with your father to make me into someone I wasn't and have no desire to be."

"No deal has been made unless you want one. I suggested it to give you an opportunity to achieve the things you want out of life." She'd wanted to hand him his dream on a silver platter. She'd imagined he'd fall over with gratitude, adoration, and love. But no, the only love in the room was on her end. For her naïveté, she deserved his scorn, as well as her own.

"I already have everything I need," he said with deathly quiet.

He turned and marched out of her trailer…and out of her life.

• • •

"You were right." Veronica stood at the front door of Ron's house. "I should have gone back to my parents as soon as I came into town."

She wanted to pretend everything was okay, that she was a flighty airhead who'd buckled under the strain of hard work. Her plan had been to smile and laugh as she said it, not have her eyes fill with tears. She'd spent a day and a half alone in her trailer hugging Matt's T-shirt and trying to get herself under control. She shouldn't have had any tears left.

Ron's eyes narrowed. "What happened?"

"You know, I broke a nail." She held up her hands, still scraped from working the outdoor jobs but healing enough that they didn't need to be bandaged.

"Come inside," Ron said gruffly, leaning on his cane as he backed out of the doorway.

She stepped into his house. It was decorated with dark wood paneling, a single brown recliner, a coffee table littered with books and newspapers, a jumbo flat-screen TV, and smelled distinctly of cigars and aftershave.

"What did he do to you?" Ron demanded, closing the door behind her.

"What? M-Matt?" She stumbled on his name. "Nothing." She rubbed her hands up and down her arms. "I quit, like you wanted me to. I couldn't take the work anymore."

"You go back there, and you stick with it," Ron said.

"No, it's over. You know I have other plans now. Matt was the only reason for me to stay with Kortville Construction." And now she didn't have any reason to be there at all. She bit her lip and blinked rapidly.

"Did you tell him all the work you did to prove the partnership needed to be dissolved and help him get his business back?" Ron asked.

"Actually, I did. He wasn't happy about that, either."

"Not happy that you were handing him his dream?" Ron sounded appalled. "What's wrong with that man? If he doesn't want my half of the partnership, I'll give it to you."

"No, I don't want it. I really don't." She shuddered to think of how much more Matt would hate her if Ron did that, if it was even possible for Matt to hate her more than he already did.

Ron set his cane aside and limped toward her. "What happened between you and Matt? Did he hurt you?"

She shook her head but had to press her fist against the ache in her heart. "He just has a different vision for his life." One that didn't include her, not even on the periphery.

"You know, I'm still half owner," Ron said. "I could take out some big loans, underprice a bunch of jobs, buy a lot of equipment he can't afford, and basically run the business into the ground…and *then* sign it over to him."

"No, please." She reached out and squeezed his hands

to make him understand this was much too serious for his games. "Matt's worked so hard to make his business a success. I know you bailed him out at the beginning, but he does all the work. He deserves to have it belong to him."

Ron stared into her eyes. "You fell in love with him, and that jerk broke your heart, didn't he?"

There was nothing else to add. Ron had summed it up exactly. She looked away and tried to pull her hands free. "It doesn't matter."

"It matters. Love always matters." He kept a tight hold on her hands. "Come into the kitchen. I have a pot of coffee on."

She finally got her hands free and followed him into another room with dark paneling and twenty-year-old appliances. He nudged her into a chair and set a steaming cup in front of her.

"So tell me what happened?" Ron pulled out the chair across from her and sat down.

"Nothing. You know us flighty types. We give our hearts away too quickly. They're easily broken and just as easily mended." She attempted a breezy tone, but her throat was so thick with tears that she failed miserably. She cupped her hands around the hot mug and stared into its murky depths.

She'd tried to turn off her love for her parents and pretend she didn't care as she walked out on them. It hadn't worked. In less than two weeks, they'd been fully back in her life. She'd have less success living in the same town as Matt, watching him continue his day-to-day life. After making such a show of her so-called willpower, she'd gone and done what she'd promised she wouldn't do. She'd depended on someone else to fulfill her and make her happy.

Ron tipped her chin up, so she was forced to look at him. "You were right when you stood up to me and pointed out you deserved a lot more respect than I was giving you. I think

Matt could use the same slap on the head."

She lifted her mug to her lips, even though her throat wasn't capable of swallowing. She hadn't come here to bash Matt. "I'm going to stay in town and base my consulting business here. My trailer's scheduled to be torn down on Monday, and I promised Barney I wouldn't be living in it when the bulldozer showed up. I'm looking for another place to stay with dirt cheap rates until I can afford something decent."

"I'll pay your rent. I'll buy you a whole darn house," Ron said, sloshing coffee over the lip of his mug onto the tabletop.

"I don't want your money. I'm asking for information on available vacancies in town."

"You could, uh"—he cleared his throat and concentrated on wiping up the spill—"stay here until you find another place. Your mother's old bedroom is empty."

She stared at him until he finally looked up. "What about the bathroom sharing problem?"

"I could probably handle one bottle of your girlie lotions sitting around—two, max. I'll pound on the door and yell at you if you take too long, but I promise not to ground you. I learned my lesson with Angela."

Veronica hadn't thought she'd ever smile again, but a watery one found its way to her lips. "Can I call you Grandpa, too?"

Now Ron looked like he might cry. "You have a deal."

• • •

Matt spent the next couple days working on various job sites, avoiding the office, and keeping himself too busy to think. He had no idea if Veronica was around or not, but he hadn't seen her, so he figured the odds were not. Wednesday he spilled his water jug while replacing a broken window downtown, so he headed to the grocery store for a Gatorade.

The bench where the Hollisters sat was empty, stopping him in his tracks and making him scan up and down the sidewalk. The weather was beautiful, the kind of day they normally wouldn't miss. He went in the store and picked out a bottle. While Becca rang up the total, he fished his debit card out of his pocket.

She held up the card and squinted at his name. "I'm going to need to see some ID with this."

"I beg your pardon?" The Hollisters weren't outside, and now the grocery store needed to see ID. He felt like he'd stepped into an alternate universe.

"Driver's license or state ID."

He hadn't heard wrong. She just didn't make any sense. "Becca, it's Matt. I've known you since you were in diapers."

"It's store policy for anyone we don't know or seems suspicious."

"You think I'm suspicious?" Maybe she'd suffered a stroke. She was certainly acting suspicious.

"If you're going to act belligerent, I can call the manager," she said.

He'd known the manager since kindergarten, but he humored her and pulled out his license. Obviously, she was having a bad day. He'd have to ask around and see if anyone else had received the same rude treatment. She swiped his card, and he took the Gatorade to his truck. As he opened the door, he noticed the Hollisters standing in front of the Laundromat shooting the breeze. He'd run over and see if they knew what was up with Becca.

They stopped talking as he approached, which was a little strange. They'd always been perfectly congenial and forthcoming before. Maybe he was getting paranoid. "Hey, the bench by the store was empty. I was worried about you two."

"We're fine," Wilbur assured him. "We have stuff to do now. We can't lounge all day."

"Ah, the community needs thing. Veronica not only convinced you to give her the space, she also put you to work." He wasn't surprised. It took every ounce of his control not to blindly follow her with his mouth hanging open. "How's it going? I can help with some shelving or rods to hang clothes and give you a chance to sit and rest."

"Kortville Construction put all that in already."

Matt blinked. His company? In the past three years, there wasn't a single job that he hadn't overseen. If he wasn't doing the work, he was assigning it to one of his employees. And he hadn't done a thing in the Laundromat. "I'll pop my head in and take a look."

"Now's not a good time," Agatha said.

"No, definitely not." Wilbur shifted so he was squarely in front of the door.

Something was up. Matt looked through the building's large glass windows. The door to the back room was open, and he could see Veronica leaning against the frame. She appeared to be talking to someone else in the room. She smiled and laughed, her face as bright and animated as ever. He envied and resented her at the same time. He'd barely been able to function since their argument Saturday morning, and she was *laughing*.

"Who's in there with her?" Matt demanded.

The couple exchanged a look that could only mean it was a man. Matt reached around the mayor and pulled open the door. He ignored their shouts as he strode through the row of washers and dryers.

Veronica turned toward the ruckus. Emotions ranging

from hope to unbearable sadness flitted across her features before she held up a hand to her elderly saviors chasing him down. "It's okay, you guys. I can handle him." She switched her gaze to Matt. He must have imagined the emotions because now she simply looked resolved. "What are you doing here?"

"I thought I'd check on my company's progress on the community center."

"Come in and look around," she said, as if he was a friendly acquaintance she had no history with. "You'll be happy to know Ron stepped up to take on his share of the business load."

So she'd gone to Ron instead of him. That stung. He might have rejected the big city job she'd tried to push on him, but he'd have donated the labor for this project if she or anyone else had asked.

"And Toby is the hardest working boy I've ever seen. I was just telling the police chief that he definitely hasn't been out causing trouble on the town, because he's been right here pounding nails and making sure the shelves are exactly level."

"And thank goodness for that, because they were crooked enough that kids would have mistaken them for slides when you were trying to set them up!" Connor O'Malley teased as he stepped out of the shadows to stand next to Veronica.

"Is she trying to talk her way out of another ticket?" Matt tried to joke.

Connor looked at him as if he'd caught him handing out illicit substances to Jenny and her friends.

"We're trying to brainstorm ways to help keep Toby occupied this summer. Becca is really stressing out that too much time and an unsavory group of friends could add up to trouble," Veronica said.

"Ah, that explains what's going on with Becca. She had me show ID in the grocery store a few minutes ago. She said

I was acting suspicious. I thought she was losing her mind."

"And now you're loitering in the Laundromat," Connor said. "This is very suspicious behavior indeed. Did you turn in that library book yet?"

"Yes, and Veronica can vouch for me." What the hell was going on?

"You don't have any memory of a library book, do you?" Connor asked her, with a twinkle in his eye. "I think I should take him down to the station for questioning. What do you say?"

Veronica didn't smile back. She simply shook her head and bit her lip. "Let it go, Connor. He didn't do anything wrong. I'll catch up with you Saturday night." She put her arms around him in a quick hug. "If you see Toby, make sure he knows I have a place of honor reserved for him."

Connor squeezed her shoulder. "You got it, babe."

She walked past Matt without looking at him and out of the Laundromat, the glass door chiming in her wake.

"Babe?" Matt repeated, incredulous. "You're not her type."

Connor's hand clenched at his side. "If you don't get a clue soon about who her type is, I'm going to stuff you in one of these boxes and ship you off to some community that's short on construction workers so she doesn't have to put up with running into you for the rest of her life."

"Veronica's not going to stay here." Of all the things he was unsure of, he was confident of that much.

"Yes, she is. If I'm lucky, she'll eventually marry me, and we'll have a kid or two or ten."

"I thought you were stuck on Becca."

"And I thought you were a smart guy. Guess we were both wrong. Loiter in here all you want—I'm not wasting my time locking you up." Connor stormed out the same way

Veronica had.

Matt had expected after their fight on Saturday that she'd have left and he'd never see her again. But she was still here. What if she followed through with what she'd told him all along, that she planned to make this her permanent home?

What if that permanent home was the farmhouse and she would have welcomed him and Jenny to join her? He'd been trying so hard to do what his brother would have wanted, but he couldn't imagine anything Steve and Leah would have wanted for him more—his dream family with him in his dream house. And if he were going that far, he had to ask himself, why wouldn't Steve want him to turn Kortville Construction into his dream job, as well?

There was no mistake. If his brother were here, he would be horribly disappointed with the mess Matt had made of his life.

Chapter Twelve

Veronica was out of her trailer by Monday, but permits and scheduling delayed the demolition until Thursday. She stood outside the convenience store, clutching the planter of flowers she'd forgotten when she'd moved out, and watched as the backhoe dug through the trailer wall. She took a shuddering breath as the digger's claw swung around and tossed the remains of her home into the waiting dump truck.

Pauline stood next to her and squeezed her shoulder. "I know it's hard."

Barney's dog rubbed against her opposite knee, as if sharing the sentiment.

"It shouldn't be." She reached down and scratched the dog behind the ears. She, more than anyone, recognized that people made the place, not the buildings. Yet the only building she'd made tangible progress on in her whole life was being torn to shreds, and her heart ripped along with it.

"Come inside." Barney flanked her and squeezed his fleshy arm around her waist. "Doughnuts are on me today."

The thought of doughnuts brought back fresh reminders of last Saturday morning with Matt. She knew she had to move on, but the wounds were too fresh. Seeing him the other day in the Laundromat had been more than she could bear. She'd hardly held it together in front of him, and even then she'd had to dump him on Connor and dash out.

Veronica set the planter outside the door, gave the pooch another scratch on the head, and walked in with Barney. She looked around at his almost finished snack-shop hangout. "Your remodeling turned out beautiful. What do you need to finish it up? Another coat of paint and to hang the fixtures?"

"That's right. You have a good eye for construction projects. A company from Dentonville is supposed to call me with a quote on how much it'll cost to finish it, but if they're too high, I might call you."

Her heart jumped to her throat. "What happened to Matt? Why isn't he finishing it?"

"Honey, I fired him. After the way he treated you, the only thing he's ever getting out of me is dusty doughnuts and melted ice cream."

"Everything here is ready for tonight. Darling, you need to go home and soak in a nice long bubble bath and get yourself ready," Mother said.

Veronica looked around at what had once been the empty storage room in the back of the Laundromat. Now it was filled with castoff clothes of every size. Neatly stacked rows of shoes and boots lined the floor. Boxes of diapers, laundry detergent, and new packages of underwear and socks sat on the back shelf.

She wasn't sure what they would do when the initial supply ran out, but for the moment, Kortville had an amazing assortment of clothing and staples. The food pantry section would be up and running in another month, but her parents had offered to spring for a grand opening party now. They'd provided champagne, a chocolate fountain, and a stunning dessert tray. All of it was sitting out, ready for the guests to devour.

"Right." She looked around. Despite her preparations, something was missing on the inside. Her heart wasn't in it.

"Are you worried he's going to show up tonight and ruin things?"

She didn't pretend not to know who Mother was talking about. "He should show up. He has as much right to be here as anyone else. I'm more worried about other people trying to keep him away or causing a scene when he does arrive."

She was haunted over the fact that she'd cost Matt the remodeling job. She'd tried to reason with Barney, but all she'd gotten was the promise he'd pay for the work that had already been done. He refused to budge on letting Matt finish the job, and he certainly wasn't going to give Matt a good word-of-mouth recommendation.

Mother and Dad glanced at each other. "Should we tell her?" Mother asked.

"Tell me what?"

Dad hesitated. "My people liked the proposal you put together for the new building. They wanted to bring Matt in for talks, which was more a formality than anything. They were ready to sign on the dotted line. He wasn't interested. He flat-out refused to talk to us."

Dad seemed shocked, but she wasn't the least surprised. He'd hated her idea. For that matter, he'd hated her for proposing it. "At least you thought it was worth considering. Thanks, Dad, for believing in me."

"I don't just believe in you. I want to see more."

"More?"

"My vice presidents have demanded we consult you to make the most out of our investment and not trip ourselves up on unnecessary expenses while we build and move. I also know a lot of people in the city who could use a business consultant before they make big changes of their own. If you move home, I can start you off with at least a dozen referrals."

Her heart pressed against her chest at his olive branch. "I don't know if you're familiar with this little thing called technology. All I need is a computer, a phone, and Internet access, and I can work from anywhere."

Dad chuckled. "All right then. Name your rate and your hours. As soon as you set out that shingle, we'll be knocking on your door."

"The shingle's out." Hanging over her mother's bedroom in her grandfather's house.

Her father had finally hired her. She was going to have a steady paycheck. Her brand-new business was up and running. And she was in control of her career and her future.

"Are you sure about starting your business here and living here?" Mother asked.

"Yes." She was settling down in a town that welcomed her, embraced her, and respected her. She had friends she could turn to in a pinch, parents who would wing a case of champagne her way for any occasion, and a grandfather who'd opened his heart and his home to a granddaughter he'd never known. She adored them all. "It's the perfect atmosphere to work on a personal basis with my clients."

She had everything she'd ever wanted out of life.

And she was miserable.

Dad clenched his fist. "Will you take offense if I say you already got a little too personal with your first client?"

"Matt wasn't a client." She didn't try to dispute the rest of his statement. She couldn't take offense, either, not when she'd come to the same heartbreaking conclusion.

Mother looked at her speculatively. "Will you be able to live in the same town, crossing paths with him all the time?"

"Yes." She said the word with more confidence than she felt. But this town was both their homes. Even if they didn't belong together, they both belonged here.

"I'm sorry it didn't work out."

"I tried too hard to impress him, when I should have listened to what was in his heart, instead of assuming that I already knew."

Well, now she knew. He wasn't interested in her heart. Too bad she couldn't ask him to return it.

. . .

"Let's sit in a booth," Jenny said.

Matt stepped into the diner and followed her, not registering anything about the restaurant. Tonight was the open house to show off the new community needs center, and he knew Veronica was going to dazzle everyone.

"Can we see the community center before we go home?" Jenny asked. "Veronica said if I stopped by, I might see my clothes hanging there."

"When did you talk to her?" His chest ached that he'd missed an opportunity to be in her presence.

"She stopped by Miss Glenda's with another pair of shoes for Stephanie and took a bunch of Glenda's old stuff away." Veronica was a part of Jenny's babysitter's life now. Jenny continued before he could comment on it or redirect the conversation. "When can she and I have another girls' day? I asked her, and she said she'd love to, but I had to ask you."

He glanced around for Pauline to save him from answering by bringing their orders. Her gaze skirted over him from behind the cash register, and he signaled with a wave. "Just the special, Pauline."

"She likes to be with me, and you like to be with her, too," Jenny continued. "So why can't she be part of our family?"

"Because your mom and dad trusted me to raise you, not anyone else." Except that didn't ring true. He'd originally planned to do it with Kimberly by his side.

"You always say the entire town is helping me grow up," Jenny said. "And Veronica's part of our town."

She certainly was. In fact, she'd made the town more hers than his in the past week. He couldn't imagine that Steve and Leah wouldn't have 100 percent supported her efforts.

Pauline slapped a platter of six mini-espresso cups in front of him. "I'll be back in a minute with a pad of paper to rate your responses." She spun away.

"What?" But she was already gone.

Jenny giggled. "Give her perfect tens, Uncle Matt. Don't forget."

"I won't forget." Even if the cups were full of stems and seeds, he wouldn't lower the score by a single decimal. But he also didn't want to be an espresso guinea pig. He'd come to the diner to eat a meal.

"I'll have the special," he called again, as Pauline grabbed a stapled packet of paper from the counter.

"You don't like espresso?" she demanded as she approached their table.

"I like it fine, but I'd also like to eat the daily special with a glass of milk."

She confirmed Jenny's grilled cheese and then swung away, dropping a two-inch-thick packet next to the espresso tray and leaving Matt to talk to Jenny about her favorite topic again. Veronica. As much as he hated to admit it, she was his favorite topic, too.

The door to the diner swung open, and Ron walked in. He nodded to Pauline and then headed straight to Matt's table.

"Jenny, can you come to the counter and help me get this sushi ready for the community center tonight?" Pauline called.

"Can I, Uncle Matt?" Jenny jumped at the chance, sliding out of the booth before he could answer.

He watched her skip across the restaurant. Whatever Ron wanted to say to him wasn't fit for a child's ears. He knew it. Pauline knew it. Everyone else in the diner knew it.

Ron slid into the seat Jenny vacated without waiting for an invitation. He grimaced as he leaned against the table and bent his knee to fit in. "I left my cane in the car. I was afraid I wouldn't be able to resist the temptation to beat you with it if I brought it inside."

"I'll count my blessings, then," Matt said drily. "I assume you're not here to shoot the breeze."

"I've been talking to my lawyer and the company lawyer and some other hotshot lawyer that my daughter recommended who charges an arm and a leg." He pushed the espresso tray out of the way and dried the spot with a napkin.

Matt's stomach filled with dread. "What's the problem?"

"Here you go." He slapped a file folder on the table. "It's all yours. Everything's in there."

"I have no idea what you're talking about."

"Look, then." Ron shoved the folder at him irritably.

Matt opened it slowly. Three lawyers made for a lot of gobbledygook language to wade through.

"Kortville Construction is all yours again," Ron said before he'd made any sense of the legalese. "It says I have no claim on your company. The hours you worked for the past three years paid off the original investment I'd made. It's yours to do with as you wish. I'm not your partner anymore."

"I didn't ask for this," Matt said.

"I know. That's why I didn't ask your opinion before I went ahead and did it. You would have refused because, according to you, the only reason I'd do something for the town is if I'm still your partner."

"I never meant it as an insult."

"Well, trust me, I took it as one. But that makes us fair, because my opinion of you isn't going to generate goodwill for anyone. In fact, if it were up to me, I'd have kept the partnership long enough to destroy the company and bring you to your knees."

"How could you consider doing that to my brother's legacy?"

"Steve?" Ron looked shocked. "This isn't his company anymore. You made it your own. You run it differently than he did—I dare say better, which is why you were able to buy out my investment so quickly and put yourself back in the black. Steve would have been proud. And he would have wanted it all returned to you."

Matt sat, stunned. Kortville Construction was his, not something he was carrying on for someone else. Steve and Leah were gone, and now it was time for him to create his own legacy. For the first time, he didn't feel guilty considering it.

"Anyway, I got off track," Ron said. "Veronica didn't agree with my sense of justice. She wanted you to have what she thought you deserved. So I signed the papers, because it was what she wanted—not as a favor to you."

"Why is she still going out of her way to fix things for me?" It made no sense, not after the way he'd treated her.

Ron shoved himself to his feet. "There's no reasoning with someone who's in love. Since you won't give her what she really wants, all I can do is try to make up for it by giving her second best."

Matt's head was spinning. Someone in love? Veronica. In love with him. He wanted it too much to allow himself to believe he was making the right connection.

"Enjoy." Pauline came back and set his plate in front of him.

"It's liver and onions." He stared at the disgusting mass on his plate, while Jenny crawled back into the booth and happily dug into her grilled cheese and Ron marched across the restaurant.

"It's what you ordered," Pauline said with a smirk.

"But—" He shoved his plate away. "What's going on? You know I hate this dish, and you can barely keep a straight face you're so pleased with yourself. Becca at the grocery store made me show identification with my debit card when she's known me her entire life. Barney gave me a box of melted ice cream when I tried to go inside the convenience store. And you—"

He shook his head. Everyone in the whole town was conspiring against him—except Veronica, who for some bizarre reason had started championing his cause.

Pauline leaned her elbows on the table, filling his vision with her no-nonsense expression. "We don't take kindly to anyone hurting one of our own around here."

"What are you talking about? I haven't hurt anyone." He'd only *thought* about ripping Connor apart limb for limb when he'd called Veronica "babe."

"You broke Veronica's heart." Pauline looked as serious as he'd ever seen her, as she tapped her knuckles on the taste-testing paperwork. "I expect every line in this packet to be filled in before you leave your spot in this booth."

He opened his mouth but couldn't make a sound come out. Veronica. Everything revolved around Veronica. He wasn't surprised she'd worked her way into everyone's hearts. She'd done it to him, too. He couldn't resent her for taking his place inside the town's embrace and pushing him to the outside. She deserved the town's love.

What blew him away was that she cared about him. Not just him—she cared about everyone she met. And she'd convinced Ron, who now clearly hated him, to give him the one thing he could admit he wanted more than anything, now that he'd made peace with Steve and Leah's memory. If he believed what Ron and Pauline were telling him, he'd have to conclude she loved him, even though she'd never said the word to his face.

The thought of her loving him seemed like the most illogical, far-fetched notion he could dream up. Yet that's what he had thought about the idea of her growing to like life in this town, about her staying for a month, about himself falling in love with a woman like her.

The door to the diner opened, and Pauline shoved away from his table to greet the people who had just entered—Veronica's parents.

"Is the sushi ready?" Mrs. Jamison asked.

"Yes, Jenny was just helping me with the finishing touches." Pauline walked behind the counter, while Jenny jumped up and ran over to greet Veronica's mother.

That left Matt still sitting rooted in the booth, and Veronica's father glaring daggers at him. He wiped his hands on a napkin and stood up. "Mr. Jamison, may I have a word with you?"

Mr. Jamison grunted.

Matt figured it was as close to an assent as he was going to get. He took a step toward the back of the room for privacy, but Mr. Jamison didn't follow. *All right.* If he was going to say what he had to say in front of this man, he might as well say it in front of anyone else who wanted to listen in. If he had a sliver of a chance at regaining what he'd already thrown away, he couldn't let his pride stand in the way.

"Your daughter Veronica is an amazing person."

"But still not good enough for you, huh, Shaw?"

He closed his eyes briefly. "Too good for me. She went to a lot of trouble to create an opportunity for my company. I'd never seen anything like it before, and I didn't know what the hell to do with it."

"So you turned it down. Bad move."

Oh boy, this man sure knew how to make him sweat. "Yeah, it was a bad move, not just for my business. If it's too late for me to change my answer and accept the job, I'll get over it and move on. But what I didn't see when she proposed it was that she'd offered a lot more than a business deal. She'd offered me her heart."

"And you stomped on it," Mr. Jamison said, sounding like he'd enjoy personally doing the same to Matt.

He'd deserve it. His stomach clenched, knowing he'd hurt her. "I don't have an excuse, except that I can promise it won't happen again. I love your daughter, sir. And I'd like your blessing for when I walk into the Laundromat tonight and announce it to her and everyone else there."

"That's quite a plan you have." Mr. Jamison sounded more skeptical than impressed.

Matt tried to ignore that his knees were starting to shake. "It's not much of a plan. I just decided it thirty seconds ago."

"Then how do you know it's the right one?"

"Because I love your daughter." He didn't tremble a bit when he said the words. Love gave him the courage to continue. "And she loves this town as much as I do. If I'm going to have a fighting chance to get her to forgive me, I need the whole town to help me convince her." A town that was against him.

Mr. Jamison watched him silently for a moment. "If you change into some clothes that reflect your respect for my daughter, you can bring the sushi," he said as if he were doing Matt a giant favor. "But everything else is up to Veronica."

. . .

Tonight was her night to show off the spectacular generosity of the Kortville community. Overdressed in a blue floor-length cocktail gown that covered her right shoulder and then curved diagonally, keeping her left shoulder bare as well as much of her back, Veronica weaved among the townspeople popping the corks on the ridiculously expensive champagne and pretended the night was everything she'd dreamed of.

And it was. She had a business of her own, charity work she adored, a community she was an integral part of, and a family that loved her and was looking out for her best interests.

A murmur went through the crowd. She looked around and realized her parents were back. "Sushi's here," she called. "I know a lot of you didn't get a chance to sample it at the town picnic because we ran out early, so now's your chance. Pauline made extras so we'll have plenty this time."

"I helped make them, too," Jenny piped up, squeezing between the townspeople to Veronica's side.

"Hi, Jenny." She bent down to hug the girl who had captured her heart as much as Matt had. If she was here, Matt had to be nearby, even if she hadn't seen him yet.

"You think bringing sushi is going to get you special treatment from our town?" someone demanded. A murmur of agreement slithered through the gathering.

Veronica straightened and steeled her defenses. Then she realized the crowd wasn't turning hostile on her. They were circling around someone standing in the doorway. Her parents were off to the side, so they weren't the cause. But too many people between her and the doorway prevented her from seeing who had caused the commotion. She waded into the crush of bodies.

"This is her special day, and I swear if you try to ruin it, I'll have disturbing the peace charges brought against you so fast that your head will spin." Veronica recognized Connor's voice this time.

"Nobody's going to ruin anything. What's going on?" Veronica finally managed to push her way through far enough to see Matt trying to enter the doorway while Barney and Connor blocked his path.

"Take these and be on your way." Barney grabbed a pack of diapers from the shelf behind him and thrust them at Matt.

Veronica took the package and returned it to its slot. "Let him in. He brought the sushi." Although why he was carrying the platter instead of Pauline or her parents, she couldn't fathom.

"You look amazing," Matt whispered, not taking a step forward.

She caught her breath at the emotion in his gaze. He couldn't look at her that way, not if she was going to keep her sanity. Dressing like this was another reminder that she would never be the type of woman he wanted by his side on a permanent basis.

Too bad he was perfect for her.

She did a double take, realizing he wasn't wearing his usual jeans and T-shirt. He'd dressed up in a gray suit with a blue pinstriped tie that matched her dress.

"Ron went looking for you. Did you guys talk?" she asked.

"Yes." Matt tugged on his collar. "He dissolved the

partnership, said I'd earned it and Steve would have wanted me to have it. But here's the thing. I've become partial to partnerships, even though I didn't earn and I don't deserve the one I have in mind. Yet it matters more to me than anything your grandfather could have signed over."

She stared at Matt. His face was inches from hers, his brown eyes more intense than she'd ever seen. Knees shaking, she wrapped her arms around her chest and took a step back. Her heel sank into one of the donated shoes that had been kicked out from the wall into the middle of the floor, and she wobbled.

Matt reached out, sushi sliding off the crystal platter as he placed his hand on her waist, steadying her.

"Maybe you should take your shoes off and go barefoot again," Stephanie suggested.

"We have a lot of clothing options, too," Wilbur added. "How about an orange-and-red flannel shirt?"

"No, Wilbur," someone chided.

"Some things never change, you know," Veronica said, unable to look away from Matt. "I still haven't figured out how to dress appropriately for town functions."

"These come with matching neon-yellow pants," Wilbur pointed out.

"Those do not match," six people chorused.

Matt grinned. She couldn't breathe, and he was grinning as he passed off what was left of the sushi platter to Barney, over the burly man's protests. "You couldn't be dressed more appropriately, in my opinion. But if you want to wear orange flannel, I'll change into the neon yellow and donate this suit and tie. I do have one complaint about your analysis of my business, though."

"Oh, no—you have no right to complain, mister." Glenda leaned over, shaking her finger in his face.

"What's your complaint?" Veronica tried to look away from his magnetic gaze, needing the strength of her hovering friends and family to keep her from reaching out for him.

"You forgot to consider what happens if everyone in town boycotts me because I'm the biggest jerk who ever lived."

"You certainly are," Barney shouted, popping a piece of sushi in his mouth.

"Thanks, Barney," Matt muttered drily, but his gaze didn't waver from her face as he placed a second hand on her waist. "For some reason I don't understand and apparently the peanut gallery doesn't get either, you fell in love with me when I totally don't deserve you."

She gulped against the sudden attack of nausea and busied her hands with unwinding the tie that was choking him. "I'm that obvious, huh?"

"No. If it had been obvious, I wouldn't have gone around thinking my love for you was one-sided."

She blinked, sure she hadn't understood. His hands around her waist were the only thing keeping her upright. "Can you rephrase that?"

"Looks like you two could use some lessons in communication," Agatha mused. "It's obvious to me what he's getting at."

"I love you," Matt said.

Her knees gave out, and she clung to him. "Really?"

"Really, he loves you. He announced it to your father in the diner," Pauline said, now standing behind Connor in the doorway.

"He also announced he had no excuse for stomping all over your heart," Dad added.

"And that he doesn't deserve you," Ron said.

"*That's* been obvious for days," Agatha pointed out.

"Really," Jenny said earnestly, working her way to their

side. "He loves you. I do, too."

"Well, does he have a ring to prove it?" Glenda yelled.

Matt looked around at their vocal audience and then focused on Veronica again. "I was kind of hoping we could have a few seconds of privacy…"

Veronica bit her lip, not sure if she was going to laugh or cry. "I think it's too late."

He closed his eyes briefly. "I hope you mean too late for privacy, not too late for us."

She nodded, scarcely daring to hope as he pulled a ring from his pocket, her heart pounding.

"Where's the diamond on that thing?" Barney demanded. "You need a microscope to see it."

Matt tossed the tie aside and released the top button of his shirt, gulping as he looked around. "Tough crowd you've got gathered here," he said with a nervous chuckle.

"They're kind of a package deal with me." Veronica smoothed her finger along his unshaven face.

"I'll take the full package," he assured her. "Veronica… this was my mother's ring. I'll buy you something bigger if you don't want it, but there wasn't a jewelry store close enough that would have been open for me to get there and back before the end of your party."

Veronica's sobs choked her laughter, and she swiped at her eyes. Matt was going to propose. He loved her. Their lives were independent and interdependent, making both of them richer and happier than they could ever be apart. "If you think I care what size the diamond is, you still don't know me at all."

"Are you going to propose or yammer excuses all night?" Wilbur demanded.

Matt took a deep breath. "I'm going to propose." He held up the ring between his thumb and forefinger. "Veronica, I love you, heart and soul, forever. Will you marry me?"

"Yes!" She didn't wait for him to stand up but dropped to her knees and threw her arms around him, kissing him hard. "I love you."

Jenny jumped against them, hugging them tightly. Never letting go of each other, they opened their arms to include her.

"I knew that Veronica Jamison was a keeper the moment she walked into my convenience store," Barney declared.

"The deed to the farmhouse is going to have Veronica's name on it, too," Mrs. Parker added.

"Can I be a flower girl with Jenny?" Stephanie asked.

"I'm reserving the park right now," Glenda said.

"I'm catering the wedding reception," Pauline announced. "Just wait until you all try my special mango-raspberry-lemonade-chocolate-mousse wedding cake."

"Good God, what have we gotten ourselves into?" Matt's shoulders shook with laughter. "Are you regretting not giving us privacy now?"

Veronica lifted her head just enough to look Matt in the eye. She felt like her heart was going to explode with happiness. "I'm not regretting anything, my love. I can't wait to hear everything our town wants to do to celebrate our love for each other…and for them."

Acknowledgments

So many people had a hand in helping me bring this book to life. Thanks to my husband and kids for their support, patience, and understanding while I'm following my dream instead of cooking dinner. Thank you to Chicago-North for the amazing first chapter critiques that set me on the right path. Thank you to Marilyn Brant, Erika Danou, Simone Elkeles, Karen Dale Harris, and Lisa Laing for multiple brainstorming sessions, unconditional support, encouragement, good food, great times, and the best writing retreats ever. Thank you to everyone at Entangled Publishing. I am so excited to call myself an Entangled author. Special thanks to Alycia Tornetta and to my amazing editor Stacy Abrams, whose vision transformed the potential of this story into a fabulous reality.

About the Author

Sara Daniel writes what she loves—irresistible romance, captivating small-town drama, and quirky characters. She writes to entertain and to give people hope and a belief that everything can and will turn out happily ever after.

On the personal side, she's a frazzled maid, chef, chauffeur, tutor, and personal assistant. She was once a landlord of two uninvited squirrels. She's crazy about country music and the drama of NASCAR. And she has her own happily-ever-after romance with her hero husband.

www.SaraDaniel.com
http://saradanielromance.blogspot.com
http://www.facebook.com/SaraDanielSaraShafer
http://www.facebook.com/SaraShaferDaniel
http://www.twitter.com/SSaraDaniel

Find your Bliss with these new releases...

Playing at Love by Ophelia London

When a school budget crisis forces funding to be pulled from either football or music, show choir teacher Tess Johansson finds herself going head to head with the gorgeous new football coach, Jack Marshall, the boy who broke her heart fifteen years ago. Jack took the coaching job to be closer to his young daughter, but unfortunately, he is still wildly attracted to Tess, the summer love he never forgot. Tess and Jack find themselves torn between doing what it takes to win and doing what they really want—being together.

Three River Ranch by Roxanne Snopek

Aurora McAllister shows up at Three River Ranch tired, alone, and—oh, yeah—pregnant. Cowboy Carson Granger has enough trouble in his life without adding a pregnant woman to the mix, including a marriage clause before he can inherit the ranch. Carson wants nothing to do with love or marriage and especially not children...but he soon realizes Rory could be exactly what he needs. Of course, love arrives on your doorstep when you least expect it...

Sugar Rush by Rachel Astor

Dulcie Carter runs her family's homemade sweet shop, Candy Land Confections. Then she meets Nick, a molten-hot guy, whose family happens to own the big-box candy shop in town. As their competition heats up, so do the sparks between them. Can they keep their sights on winning, when love might be the sweetest prize of all?

Lucky Break **by Kelley Vitollo**

When living the LA life becomes too much for Sidney Williams, she heads back to her small hometown. Kade, the new owner of Lucky's bar and Sidney's former best friend, is determined to bring the place back to its former glory, and the attraction between him and Sidney is a distraction he doesn't need. Now, with the possibility of her first major acting role looming, Sidney must decide if her lucky break is in Hollywood or right where she left it.